Louie & Women

OTHER BOOKS BY TODD WALTON

Inside Moves

Forgotten Impulses

Louie

TODD WALTON

Women

E. P. DUTTON, INC. • NEW YORK

Copyright © 1983 by Todd Walton
All rights reserved. Printed in the U.S.A.

No part of this publication may be reproduced or transmitted in any form or by any means, electronic or mechanical, including photocopy, recording or any information storage and retrieval system now known or to be invented, without permission in writing from the publisher, except by a reviewer who wishes to quote brief passages in connection with a review written for inclusion in a magazine, newspaper or broadcast.

Published in the United States by
E. P. Dutton, Inc., 2 Park Avenue, New York, N.Y. 10016

Library of Congress Cataloging in Publication Data
Walton, Todd.
Louie and women.
I. Title.
PS3573.A474L6 1983   813'.54   82-14714

ISBN: 0-525-24167-1

Published simultaneously in Canada by
Clarke, Irwin & Company Limited, Toronto and Vancouver

Designed by Nancy Etheredge

10 9 8 7 6 5 4 3 2 1

First Edition

For my buddy Rico,
my sister Kathleen,
my grandmother Goody,
my good friend Colleen,
and for Dorothy Pittman,
the Wizard of Ossining

Because I know that time is always time
And place is always and only place
And what is actual is actual only for one time
And only for one place
I rejoice that things are as they are and
I renounce the blessed face
And renounce the voice
Because I cannot hope to turn again
Consequently I rejoice, having to construct something
Upon which to rejoice

T. S. ELIOT

1.

Seen from the road, it appeared to be nothing more than a large, gray plastic bag that had blown out into the field and lodged among the heads of iceberg lettuce. It was, however, not a bag but a poncho, and beneath its wrinkled exterior there lay a man named Louie Cameron.

An old brown backpack served him as both pillow and windbreak, and the inflatable pad beneath him made the lumpy ground tolerable for sleep. He had a flashlight to read and write by, dried fruit and nuts to give him nourishment, and a tiny gas stove should he desire his water hot. He lacked only company, and given the dimensions of his canopy, it was not a lack that grieved him much that rainy evening.

It was April of a very wet year in California and the lettuce harvest was at its height. Louie had been picking the heads for two weeks, going into Salinas in the evenings to see movies, to eat good Mexican food and to watch the beautiful women promenade down Main Street.

In the morning, Louie would head for the coast. He had worked hard, saved a little money, and now he wanted to sit on the sand, to soak his aching feet in the cold water, to rest a while before moving on.

Marie

When I was in prison, I used to lie awake, looking at the ceiling, waiting for a certain sound that I would be sure was Louie coming to take me home. He would move like a shadow past the guards, open the door, lift me from my bed, wrap me in black silk, and carry me out into the night, without anyone knowing.

When I finished my time at Soledad and moved back to Santa Cruz, I'd lie awake in the same way. I'd wait for my children to settle into sleep and then I'd listen for an engine sound: his old Volkswagen coughing as it shifted down from third gear to second.

But I don't listen for his car anymore. Now, I wait for the dog to bark. Louie doesn't like Dobermans, so he'll stay out on the sidewalk until I come for him. I'll put on my white kimono, go downstairs, open the door and look out at him for a long time. I want to make him wait, like I've been waiting for three years now. Then I'll walk slowly down the path, stopping before I get too close. He'll be dying to come in, but the dog will be there, keeping him out.

I never get to the part where I forgive him. I can't conjure up how that will be. There's just this jumble of pictures and words and anger, so I don't know what I might do. I can't help thinking my life would have been better if he'd stayed in Santa Cruz and waited for me.

Then again, I know he couldn't have stayed. Everything he owned, everything he believed in, was taken from him because he didn't know how to fight. I've tried to hate him for leaving, but all I can hate is his leaving. Hating Louie would be like hating a child for not knowing that fire burns and things can break.

2.

The strong breeze blowing in from Monterey Bay had scattered the rain clouds and left the freshly plowed fields steaming in the morning light. Louie was walking toward Salinas, his big lumpy pack on his back, a straw hat on his head, his clompy hiking boots squeaking as they came down on the asphalt.

He stopped to watch a white egret stalking frogs in a shallow pond. Each movement the big bird made was followed by a long pause, as its yellow, unblinking eyes searched for shadows in the muck. The bird made a sudden stab at the water, then slowly lifted its head, a bullfrog wedged in its beak. Louie turned away before the egret could swallow.

A flatbed truck jammed with farm workers rumbled by on its way to the lettuce harvest. Louie was going in the opposite direction, and he couldn't help laughing as he waved to them, though there was a part of him that wished he was riding with them, feeling the strength of their company.

A swarm of finches swept across the road in front of him—little rosy blurs that solidified into birds as they lighted on the barbed wire, then dropped to the ground in search of seed. "Hi, birds," Louie said.

He passed an old, inaccurate road sign, a relic from the days before freeways. Black letters on a white background announced

SALINAS 6
SANTA CRUZ 41

A hitchhiker's addendum, scratched in with a pocketknife, read

FRISCO 100
L.A. 300

Then he thought he heard someone scream. He closed his eyes, listened hard, and it came again, from far away. Reflexively, he tightened his waist belt and started hiking. He heard the scream again, closer, and he knew it was a woman. She was articulating words. She was saying "No," and "Jesus." When Louie was very close, he heard her say, "No, Jesus, Larry, no!"

Louie slowed to a walk. He was ten yards from a narrow bridge that carried the highway over a creek.

6

The woman was under the bridge, being hurt by some-one named Larry.

Louie took off his pack, removed his hat, then took from the pack a three-foot length of heavy steel chain. He gripped it tightly, spit to exorcise his fear, then left the road and picked his way down the steep embankment to the creek.

There were two young men under the bridge with the woman. One of them lay on top of her, raping her. The other man stood watching them, his face smooth and expressionless, his eyes half-closed. The one on top of the woman was brown-haired, the watcher was blond. They both wore jeans and old work shirts, and carried knives on their belts.

It was dark under the bridge. Louie could barely see the woman beneath the man. He cleared his throat and hit the ground with his chain. The man rolled off the woman and scrambled to his feet, pushing his erect penis to one side so he could zip up his pants. The blond got his knife out, then the brown-haired one got his knife out, too.

The woman lay still for a moment, then very slowly pulled up her underwear and got to her feet. She took a few faltering steps, then she darted past the two young men, got behind Louie and scrambled up the slope to the road.

The two men started after her, but Louie blocked their way. They stopped several feet short of him, their knives pointed rigidly at him, fixed like bayonets on the ends of their arms.

"Come back, Chris," shouted the brown-haired man, a surprising tenderness in his voice. "Don't go, baby."

"Put the knives down," said Louie, tightening his grip on the chain.

7

"Forget it," said the brown-haired man, sneering viciously.

The blond man said nothing. He moved away from his companion to Louie's right. Louie compensated by taking a step backward up the incline. The brown-haired man took a step forward.

"Put 'em away or I start swinging," Louie said, loudly. "I got no time for kid's stuff."

The brown-haired man froze, looking to his partner for inspiration. "Whaddaya think, Johnny?"

Johnny said nothing. Instead, he took another step away. This meant they would fight, so the brown-haired one, Larry, dropped into a crouch and began to circle the other way around Louie.

Louie gave a quick glance at Johnny, then leaped toward Larry, swinging his chain down hard, smashing the knife out of Larry's hand. Then he whirled quickly, the chain striking Johnny square on the jaw and knocking him down. Louie whirled again, his chain humming as it cut the air. Larry was coming at him, weaponless, and the chain wrapped around Larry's throat, strangling him. Larry clutched at the steel and fell backward, jerking the chain from Louie's hand. Louie turned again to face Johnny, but too late. Johnny, on his knees, thrust his knife into the side of Louie's left leg, just below the knee, and as Louie danced away, the blade sliced down his leg, the blood oozing out like oily wine. Louie bellowed with rage, kicked the knife out of Johnny's hand, then kicked him again in the side of the head, sending him tumbling down to the edge of the creek.

Louie, his hands trembling, backed slowly up the hillside. Larry had managed to loosen the chain around his neck, but had not removed it. He lay on his back, his hands over his eyes. Johnny lay on his side, slumbering, his boyish face inclined toward Louie, a dark purple blotch on his chin.

Louie was weak and dizzy when he got up to the road. He pulled a handkerchief out of his pocket and tied it around his leg, above his knee. Then he wrestled his pack onto his back and began walking toward Salinas. He went about fifty yards, then had to stop. His leg was numb and he was starting to shiver. He took off his pack, got out a sweater and put it on, then looked down the road in both directions. An old pickup truck, toylike in the distance, was coming toward him.

He stumbled out into the middle of the road and held up his arms, though the truck was still a long way off. Louie glanced to his right and saw an endless expanse of brown fields, topped by a cloudless sky. He looked to his left and saw a huge flock of blackbirds fluttering down to the ground like heavy pieces of ash. "Nice," he whispered, turning to face the oncoming truck.

Marie

We'd been in Santa Cruz for about a year when my brother Billy dragged me down to the Seaside Inn to hear Louie play the piano. He was performing solo and Billy was all fired up to be his bass player. Billy still says Louie only agreed to take him on because of me, but I know that's not true. Louie was a perfectionist about his music.

Still, there were sparks between us, no doubt about it, and I was ready for just about anything he had in mind, but he was married and wouldn't have dreamed of cheating on his wife, though she cheated on him every chance she got. Everybody in town seemed to know about it but Louie.

Then, after he and Billy had been playing together for a few months, he started coming over for supper before they'd go off to play. He'd wrestle with Cal and cradle Eva in his arms and coo to her, and I'd ache for him to love me like that. Cal was two and a half, Eva was almost a year old, and they both took to him right away.

I sometimes think if Louie hadn't been so good with my children I could have left him alone, waited for him to get out of his marriage before I chased him. I was so hungry then, for all sorts of things, but mostly for love, and Louie seemed to gush the stuff. It was in his music, his voice, his eyes, the way he moved. He wasn't like any man I'd ever known, and I wanted him.

3.

As Louie regained consciousness, a shock of pain ran up his leg, along his left side, through his armpit and out to the fingers of his left hand. He opened his eyes and looked around. He was lying on a bed in a very small, brightly lit room. An older Mexican man, wearing a white shirt and a black bow tie, was carefully prodding the skin around Louie's wound with a hypodermic needle. Another Mexican man stood at Louie's side, peering down at him.

"Gable," said Louie, the word coming out slowly. "You look just like Clark Gable."

12

"My name is Luis," said the man at Louie's side, his accent slight, his voice gruff. "I brought you here. This is Dr. Macias."

"The resemblance is uncanny," said Louie, smiling at Luis.

"What's your name?" asked Dr. Macias, his accent much thicker than Luis's.

"Louie," he said, wincing as the needle touched a nerve.

"Please try to hold still," said Dr. Macias. "This shouldn't hurt too much. The cut is long, but not so deep."

"Do you have money for the doctor?" asked Luis, coughing, his face heavy with worry.

"Hey," said Louie, laughing weakly. "Luis and Louie. Same name, different language, right?"

"Money," said Luis, leaning closer. "Do you have money for the doctor?"

"If I don't have enough, I can get it," said Louie, looking Luis in the eye.

Dr. Macias began to stitch the wound. He worked quickly, talking as he sewed. "Don't put much weight on this for a couple days and don't get it wet. There may be a little nerve damage, and a chance of infection, so I'll give you pills for the pain along with some antibiotic."

"I appreciate this," said Louie, propping himself up on his elbows to watch the doctor work.

"Thank Luis," said the doctor, tying off the last stitch, then standing up and stretching, his fingers almost touching the low ceiling. "Voy a hablar con Rosa por un momento," he said, "y después, me voy. Adiós, Luis. Good luck, Louie. Buena suerte."

"Gracias," said Louie, raising his hand to say goodbye.

13

When the doctor was gone, Luis sat on the bed beside Louie and smoked a cigarette. He looked at Louie for a few minutes without speaking, and then he laughed, which caused him to cough.

"What's so funny?" asked Louie, smiling expectantly.

"You should have seen yourself, man," said Luis, shaking his head. "You looked like a scarecrow, your arms hanging out, your head hanging down, blood all over the road. You're lucky I didn't just run you over and to hell with you."

"I'm going to pay you," said Louie, tired of saying it. "I have thirty dollars and I'll send more."

Luis blew a cloud of smoke, then dispelled it with a wave of his hand. "It's not for me, man. But I gotta stay good with the doctor. I got six kids, you know. Gotta stay good with him."

"There was a woman," said Louie, trying to sit up.

"She do that to you?" asked Luis, grimacing at Louie's leg.

"No," said Louie. "Two guys had her under the bridge."

"And you went down there?" asked Luis, dropping his cigarette to the floor and crushing it with his boot. "What if they had a gun, man?"

"You didn't see her?" asked Louie, disappointed.

"I only saw you, man."

"You really do look like Clark Gable," said Louie, smiling again. "In *The Misfits*, with Marilyn Monroe."

"I didn't see that movie," said Luis, standing up. "I'll get you some water, then you better sleep."

Louie slept into the night, but he had a bad dream and sat up shouting. A woman came into the room, in the darkness, put her hands on his shoulders, and made

14

him lie back down. She smelled of cinnamon and spoke to him soothingly in Spanish.

"Some more aspirin might help," Louie whispered, breathing hard. "Aspirina?"

"O, sí," she said, the air swirling as she moved away from him. A moment later, she returned with aspirin and milk, helped him sit up and held the glass for him as he drank.

"Gracias," he said, lying back, greatly relieved.

"Nada," she said, placing her small hand on his forehead. "Mañana."

He heard her get into bed in the next room. Then he heard Luis say, "Cómo?" and she said something about the aspirin and other things Louie couldn't hear well enough to understand.

Marie

Billy and the kids and I moved out from Texas when my husband went into prison for armed robbery. I never wanted to see him or Texas again. The only thing I've got left from there is my accent, and it's almost gone. Now and again, I'll hear a little of it from Cal when he calls to me when he comes home from school, but Eva doesn't have a shred of it.

We got to Santa Cruz before it got too posh-posh, and we rented a nice little house near the beach for pretty cheap. I put my hair in braids, left off my make-

16

up and got a job at the bakery downtown across the street from the post office. Billy got on at the cannery and played bass in a country-and-western band until he found Louie.

If *I* hadn't met Louie, I might still be working at the bakery, but I doubt it. Seeing all the wealth here, all these rich, lazy people, did something to me. I wanted money to buy nice things for my kids, to give them what I never had, and so I could have some fun, too. I was only twenty-five and I wasn't ready to sell doughnuts for the rest of my life. I hated how poor I was, how ignorant and uncultured I was, so I started taking courses at the community college and going to lectures up at the university.

I wanted to turn myself into someone elegant, somebody who traveled and knew about the world, somebody who dressed with style, drove a nice car, and knew about philosophy and art. I wanted to be rich so I could transform myself into a cultured person. I actually thought it was something I could buy, if I could just get enough money. And then, once I'd been transformed, somebody like Louie would want me.

It's funny to think back on it now, because I know Louie didn't care about any of that. He didn't really care about *things*. I can't put it into words, but I could feel what he cared about when he'd play the piano. I could hear it in the chords he chose, in the sad melodies he'd build and tear down and build again. He was so vulnerable when he played, and I know that was part of what made me love him.

17

4.

Half sunk into the soil and overgrown with blackberry bushes, the big cement pipe was an invisible sanctuary, a dry, well-ventilated cave. It sat on a knoll overlooking the Pajaro River, fifteen miles south of Santa Cruz, where the river made its last turn before meeting the sea. The pipe was six feet in diameter and twelve feet long—a dark adobe, stained with the tracks of seasonal fungus.

Louie stood storklike on his good leg, sawing at the thick brambles with his Swiss Army knife. He was tired and dizzy from his slow trek across the artichoke field and barely had the strength to cut his way through to the pipe.

"Hello?" he said, though he could see no one was there. The floor of the pipe was strewn with mouse droppings and tufts of animal hair. The walls were scratched with the names of towns and people, and with dates, the earliest being 1949. Only one lodger had taken the time to carve an entire phrase into the barely yielding stone. He'd written, "Revolution begins here." There was no sign that anyone with a feĩt pen had ever visited there.

The sky at the western end of the pipe was cloudless, but huge gray thunderheads were gathering to the east. Louie swept out the pipe, put down a tarp, unrolled his foam pad and spread out his sleeping bag. He took off his boots and pulled off his pants, checking his stitches before crawling into the sack.

Seeing the wound reminded him to take a pain pill, which he did with the last of his water. He cursed himself for not filling his canteen at Luis's. Then he lay down, closed his eyes, and fell into a feverish sleep, from which the ensuing storm, fierce as it was, could not rouse him.

Marie

Sometimes we'd stay up talking all night. It always started out the three of us, then Billy would cash it in, and Louie and I would be alone. The first few minutes after Billy was gone were always a little awkward, but then I'd get out the brandy and things would loosen up. Louie would tell me about his life and I'd tell him about mine, and I'd try to get him to talk about his marriage, but he usually wouldn't, because he didn't believe in talking about Joanna behind her back.

He'd get all worked up about architecture and tell

me what he'd do if they'd only give him the money and turn him loose. He hated the grunt work he had to do for the firm, loved to design, but he'd only been the principal architect on one job, and it wasn't something he could be real creative with. By the time I met him, he was just putting in his time at the office, waiting for the days to end so he could get to his music.

He wanted to leave his wife, I know he did, and I think if they hadn't owned the house together, splitting up wouldn't have been so hard. But they'd bought it together, fixed it up together, put all their love into it, and *it* was still standing, even if their relationship wasn't.

He loved the house. I remember him taking me through the first time, showing me all the changes he'd made, telling me all the things he still wanted to do. I listened hard and didn't forget any of it, because I knew he was talking about himself, and I wanted to know everything about him.

When she asked for a divorce, she told him about her lovers, how she'd done it with them everywhere in the house while he was at work. She knew that would sicken him more than plain adultery. She knew it would make him hate the house so he would agree to let her have it.

I could see what she'd done, and after Louie told me, all I could think about was going over there and getting his house back for him.

21

5.

Louie reached for his canteen before he was awake enough to remember it was empty. His throat was parched, his lips were cracked, his leg was throbbing. He called himself a fucking moron, then tried to muster enough saliva to swallow a pain pill, but he was dry as a bone. The pill stuck at the back of his mouth, and he had to spit it out before he gagged.

He ate some dried fruit and pondered the situation. He had to get water and he had to pee. Eventually, he would be forced to get up, but he wanted to delay that for as long as possible. He rummaged in his pack and found a small bottle of apricot brandy with just enough of the sticky stuff left to take his pill and soothe his throat.

Emerging from the pipe a half-hour later, Louie squinted up at the bright, cloudless sky, then turned full circle to see where the thunderheads had gone. They were far out to sea, a barely visible armada on the horizon.

Louie was only a few hundred yards from the ocean, but he could neither see nor hear the surf because of the intervening sand dunes. There was drinking water on the dunes, piped in from Watsonville to the beach houses. He would rather have taken his water from the river, but it was so heavily polluted with insecticides and chemical fertilizers, no amount of boiling could make it safe to drink. He would have to traverse the dunes and get to the houses from the beach, since the inland access was blocked by a gate and security guards.

Limping through the field and along the road to the dunes didn't take him long, but he had to crawl on his hands and knees to make any progress going up the dune. His canteen dangled from his neck and swayed from side to side, causing the canvas strap to saw into his skin. By the time he reached the top of the dune, he was sweating and breathing hard, but the sight of the ocean revived him, and he hooted for joy.

The offshore wind stung him with fine particles of grit. As he averted his face, he saw the condominiums to the north—four ugly cement towers, wedged between artichoke fields and the ocean. He looked to the south where the beach houses were clustered, then he closed his eyes and breathed deeply.

He decided to limp down the dune to the beach, so he crawled a few yards further, then sat with his legs out in front of him, pointing downhill. He lay back, rocked forward and lurched up onto his good leg. But his momentum was too great and he toppled forward, somersaulting twice before he was able to stop himself. He clutched at his leg, gripping the skin around the wound with both hands. He gritted his teeth and grunted to relieve the sudden sharp pain.

He considered making his way back to the pipe, but he knew he couldn't do without water, so he crawled down to the beach, where the sand was wet and hardpacked. On solid ground, he stood up easily, then hopped southward until he came to a pile of driftwood. He sat on a water-worn redwood log and tried to ignore his leg while he caught his breath.

The wide, flat beach was empty of people. Dozens of sanderlings hurried about at the edge of the waves, pecking madly at the sand, while the willets, with their longer, skinnier bills, placidly probed the shallows. The sun beat down on Louie's back, and he smiled despite his discomfort.

A golden retriever rushed by in pursuit of the shore birds. The sanderlings took flight en masse, whistling as they escaped. The willets were less skittish and the dog had to get close to them before they made an effort to fly. Having vanquished the birds, the dog hunted up a stick and brought it to Louie.

"Scared my birds," said Louie, taking the stick from the dog and flipping it toward the water. The dog caught the stick in midair and pranced back to Louie with it. "Wanna go swimming?" asked Louie, pulling the stick away from the dog. He stood up and poised himself to throw, but someone shouted at him, so he restrained himself. The retriever barked impatiently, his eyes fixed on the stick.

A woman ran toward them, waving her arms. Louie smiled when he saw her face. At first glance, she resembled the young Claudette Colbert. She had curly brown hair, round rosy cheeks, big almond eyes, and baby doll lips.

"I'm sorry," she said, breathlessly. "Could you throw it *away* from the water? We just bathed him."

"Sure," said Louie, flinging the stick backward over his shoulder.

"You're bleeding," she said, moving toward him. "A lot, it looks like."

"Oh, shit," he said, looking down at himself. Blood was dripping from his pants leg onto the sand. "I must have torn out some stitches when I fell."

"I'll get help," she said, turning away from him.

"No, don't," said Louie, raising his hands in protest. "I'll be okay."

"Don't be silly," she said, starting to run.

The dog dropped his stick at Louie's feet, then chased after the woman. Louie gritted his teeth and began limping back toward the pipe. He only managed to go twenty yards before he was overcome by dizziness. He sat down on the sand and bowed his head.

Moments later, the dog returned and offered another stick to Louie. The young woman was not far behind, followed by an older woman carrying a plastic first-aid kit.

"Why did you leave?" asked the young woman, stopping several feet from Louie.

"I don't want to impose," he said, unable to look her in the eye.

"Let's carry him," said the older woman, smiling

expectantly. She was extremely skinny, fragile-seeming, with a narrow face, long white hair and very bright, green eyes.

"I don't think he wants us to," said the young woman, watching Louie's face.

"Nonsense," said the older woman, coming closer. "He's either in shock or he's one of those stupid proud people." She put a hand on Louie's shoulder and gazed intently at him. "He's harmless," she pronounced. "Let's carry him."

"I can take him on my back," said the young woman. "He's very thin, and you're not supposed to be lifting."

Louie laughed and shook his head. "This is great," he murmured. "Just great."

"What's so funny?" asked the young woman, glaring down at him.

"I had older sisters," Louie explained. "And they used to fight over me, too."

"Without asking your permission, I'll bet," said the older woman, nodding sympathetically. "My sister and I fought over our brother, too, poor boy."

The young woman gave Louie a hand up, then turned her back to him and bent over slightly. "Get on," she said, quietly.

Louie got on and she hooked her arms under his legs. He clasped his hands together around her chest, making sure not to touch her breasts.

"No problem," she said to the older woman. "He doesn't weigh a thing."

"Goodness," said the older woman, as she walked along beside them. "We haven't introduced ourselves. My name is Helen, and this is my daughter Andrea."

"My name is Louie," he said nodding. "This is very kind of you. I feel so stupid."

"Don't," said Helen, smiling at him. "Think of it as an adventure."

Louie relaxed against Andrea. He was amazed at her strength and stamina. She stopped only briefly at the bottom of the stairs that led from the beach up to the dune houses. She lifted him higher onto her back and got a better grip before ascending.

"Here, Buka," said Helen, calling to the dog.

The dog stayed on the beach, pawing the sand around his stick and whining. "Buka," said Andrea, sternly. The dog lowered his head and followed them.

"Do you need to rest?" asked Louie, speaking softly.

"No," said Andrea. "You really are frighteningly light."

"I'm sorry about this," said Louie. "I'm sure it's nothing serious."

Andrea didn't reply, but turned to watch her mother climb the last few stairs.

"I'm fine, I'm fine," said Helen, pausing for a moment before taking the last step up. "I just climbed a bit too fast."

The dog sneaked past them and trotted ahead, his toenails clicking on the narrow pedestrian boardwalk that spanned the dunes. Between the rows of houses the ocean breezes were tame, the crash of the waves muffled. Louie knew the Pajaro houses well. He'd drawn the details on several of the designs, though he'd never fulfilled his dream of building a house there.

Helen and Andrea's home was large and rustic, built of river rock and redwood, nestled between two densely vegetated dunes. The redwood had faded to gray and the wood and stone were now nearly indistinguishable.

Helen unlocked the door and the dog trotted in.

Andrea waited for her mother to come back with a rag to catch the blood dripping from Louie's leg.

"Nice place," said Louie, shifting his weight slightly. "I remember when it was built."

"You do?" said Andrea, surprised. "When was that?"

He thought for a moment. " 'Seventy-five. They finished it right before the rains came that year."

"That's right," she said, carrying him inside.

"We'll work in the kitchen," said Helen, leading the way. "Easy to mop up."

Andrea let go of Louie's legs and he slid down off her hips, but kept his hands on her shoulders as he balanced himself on one foot. Helen put a chair behind him and he sat down. Andrea turned to look at him, her face taut from the strain of carrying him. Free of her burden, she relaxed, her round cheeks softened and her dark eyes grew moist. She was taller than Louie had thought at first. Her limbs were long, her bones quite fine, and she didn't look anything like Claudette Colbert.

Louie touched his shaggy brown hair and said, "Just take a little off the sides."

Andrea smiled as she knelt in front of him. "I think we'll just take off your pants."

The stitches had torn out in two places. Blood was dripping steadily from the wound, despite the gray crust of sand and dried blood that had formed over it. Helen wiped the stitches with a wet towel and Louie growled in pain.

"I'm sorry, dear," she said, wincing sympathetically, "but we have to get it clean so we can see what we're doing. Look how skinny he is, Andrea. Heat up some soup, will you?"

"Please, don't go to any trouble," said Louie. "I'm fine."

"He's bleeding to death and he says he's fine," said Andrea, opening the refrigerator. "That's so perfectly male, don't you think?"

"Pride," said Helen, cleaning the wound with iodine. "Now what have we here?"

"Twenty-seven stitches," said Louie, trying to catch Andrea's eye. He wanted her to see him glaring at her, but she wouldn't look at him.

"Minus seven or eight," said Helen, studying the wound. "I can tie in here and here," she said, turning to Andrea. "I'll need my sewing basket."

"*You're* gonna stitch it?" said Louie, laughing nervously. "You're kidding, right?"

"She's not kidding," said Andrea, stirring the soup. "Her father was a doctor."

"I've stitched a thousand stitches," said Helen, smiling benignly. "You came to the right place. Except we don't have any anesthetic and not a drop of whiskey in the house."

Helen used a large needle and a double strand of black cotton thread, sterilized in boiling water. Louie gripped the seat of the chair as she sewed.

"I . . . I think you'd better stop," he said, hyperventilating. "I'm feeling a little faint."

"I'm nearly done, dear," said Helen. "Just be calm and you'll be fine."

"Are you . . . are you from Boston?" he asked, gasping for air.

"Yes, dear, originally. Why?"

But Louie lost consciousness before he could reply. He sagged in his chair and Helen had to move quickly to keep him from falling. "Andrea," she said calmly, "come hold him up. I have one more stitch to do."

Marie

He stood in my kitchen, looking scared and lost, saying over and over again, "She can have the house. I don't want it anymore."

Every time he'd say it, I'd get madder, until finally I grabbed him and shook him and told him I wasn't going to let her do that to him. I told him to go face up to her, but he wouldn't. He stuck his hands in his pockets and stared at the floor, like he'd done something wrong.

So I took him by the hand, led him out to his car and we drove over together. I knew it was a mistake for

30

me to go, but I was too angry to stop myself. I hated her
for what she was doing to him, and I hated her because
she was married to him.

He wouldn't get out of the car. I had to drag him
up the front walk, and even then he wouldn't look at the
house. He stood with his back to the front door and
started to cry. I should have taken him away right then,
calmed him down and made love to him, made him
forget, but I didn't think of it then because I wanted him
to be brave. If he was going to be my man, he had to be
brave. That's the way I thought then. I still had all that
Texas shit running in my veins. So I made him turn and
face the house, and then I knocked on the door. Then I
banged on it with my fist until somebody answered.

If it had been anybody but Paul Whitson, I might
have calmed down, but seeing him there just made me
even angrier. It was bad enough she was cheating on
Louie, but to be doing it with Paul Whitson made it
worse. I wanted Louie to chase the bastard away, but he
wouldn't.

Paul Whitson was one of those men who'd learned
to fake sensitivity. He pretended to care about the
downtrodden of the world, when all he wanted was to
snort coke and get laid and look at himself in the mirror.
He was always saying how much he identified with
women. He used to come into the bakery and try to get
me to go out with him, but I wouldn't even talk to him.
Then he'd go to the coffeehouse across the street and sit
around bullshitting about his organic life-style, with a
bag of chocolate chip cookies in his wicker briefcase,
along with his Karl Marx and books about spiritual
rebirth. I don't know how Joanna fell for that crap, or
maybe she didn't. Maybe she knew he was a phony and
didn't care.

Anyway, I told him to get out of the way, that

Louie had to see Joanna, but he wouldn't move. He acted like it was his house. I shouted for Joanna, but he said we'd just have to talk to her lawyer, because she wasn't going to talk to us. So I turned to Louie and shouted at him to do something, but he just stood there looking helpless. I couldn't stand seeing him like that, so I tried to push by Paul, but he shoved me back and I fell, and then before I could even think I had the knife in my hand, the way my daddy taught me, bringing it out of my pocket and clicking it open all in one movement. I never went anywhere without that knife, not since I was a kid, though in all those years I'd never used it.

And then he came at me, I know he did, because if I'd gone for him I would have hurt him, not just cut him a little. At the trial, Paul said he was going to help me up, and maybe he was, but I thought he was going to hit me, and I still think maybe he was.

I remember standing there, watching Louie hold the skin on Paul's chest together. Then Paul lost consciousness and Louie yelled at me to call an ambulance. And then Joanna came out and saw the blood, and she started screaming. Then she ran back inside to call the police. I just stood there, trying to wake up, trying to shake it off because I was sure it was a bad dream.

6.

No previous blackouts or dizziness?" asked the doctor, a big, beefy fellow with a ruddy face and sparse gray hair. He sat in a chair by the bed, his legs crossed, his right foot pumping up and down in the air.

"No," said Louie, smiling wanly. "Just these two times."

The doctor leaned close, his breath smelling of bourbon and cigars. "Don't let her take the damn things out unless I'm here. I'm just two houses down, front row. I was home." He shrugged, stood up, covered his

33

mouth and burped. "Don't move for a couple days unless you have to."

"I'd like to pay you," said Louie.

"Whatever," said the doctor, shrugging again as he turned to go.

Louie closed his eyes and was about to drift off to sleep when the door opened. A man in a wheelchair rolled into the room. Helen was pushing him and Andrea was behind them, carrying a tray of soup and bread.

"Visitors," said Helen, beaming at Louie. "This is my husband, George."

"Hello," said Louie, sitting up.

"No, no," said Helen, "stay down."

George was wearing a red tartan bathrobe and large purple mittens. His curly white hair was long and tangled, his old man's face more drawn than wrinkled. He resembled Mark Twain in old age. An unlit pipe hung loosely from the corner of his mouth, but it must have been wedged under his upper teeth because his lips were not holding it. His clear brown eyes were unfocused, and though he was facing Louie, he did not seem to be seeing him.

"He's recently had a stroke," said Helen, sitting at the foot of the bed, facing her husband. "I think it's best to act as if he's capable of understanding you." She turned to Louie and patted his foot through the covers. "I'd appreciate that, and who knows, he might appreciate it, too."

"Sure," said Louie, looking expectantly at George.

"Louie's going to be our guest for a few days, dear," she said, turning back to her husband.

"Thank you very much," said Louie, speaking to George.

A silence followed. Andrea shifted uncomfortably

34

and looked at the floor. Helen reached out, touched her husband's hands and said, "Now we have a third for hearts." Then she stood up, turned George's chair around and pushed him out of the room.

Andrea moved to the bedside with the tray of food. She put another pillow behind Louie so he could sit up more easily, then she set the tray on his lap and stepped back.

"We didn't ask you if you *wanted* to stay," she said, looking at her hands as if she'd just discovered something awful about them, "but you really should. We're set up for board and care anyway."

"I have a camp," said Louie, dipping the bread in his soup. "It's just on the other side of the river. I could stay tonight, then tomorrow . . ."

"Tell me where it is," she said, moving to the edge of the bed. "I'll go get your stuff. You should stay off your leg for a few days at the very least."

Louie smiled. "I've been trying to get your accent but I couldn't quite figure it all out until just now."

"What do you mean?"

"Well, I knew your mother was from Boston, and you've got a slight drawl, which means you've been living in the South, but not the deep South, Virginia or North Carolina, but there was something else. The way you just said 'board and care' and 'at the very least,' was definitely British. So either your father is from England or you went to school there when you were little."

"Why when I was little?" she asked, unzipping her sweatshirt, revealing a red University of Virginia T-shirt.

"There was no affectation in the way you said it," Louie said, looking up from the T-shirt to her face.

"I was born in Boston," she said, nodding, "and we moved to England when I was four. We stayed there

35

until I was twelve, and then we moved back to Boston." She backed up a few steps and leaned against the wall. "I've lived all over the world since I left home, but I've been teaching at the University of Virginia for five years now."

"What subject?"

"Drawing and Art History," she said, smiling slightly. "I'm surprised you didn't guess that, too."

"I'm good at guessing where people have been, but not what they do," said Louie, looking at his soup. "This is delicious, by the way."

"You're a big surprise," she said, putting her hands behind her back. "Here I thought you were just a bum."

"Oh, I *am* a bum," said Louie, stirring his soup and nodding. "This really is good. Thank you."

"You're welcome," she said, moving to the door "Call me if you want anything more."

When she was down the hall and out of earshot, Louie said quietly, "I want to be better looking, more intelligent and much happier. A good dark beer would be nice, too."

Andrea

As bedraggled as he was,
there was something very appealing about him. There
was also something very familiar about him, as if I'd
known him when we were younger. But try as I might,
I couldn't think of anyone he really reminded me of.

When I came back into his room to take away the
lunch tray, he was asleep, his elbow stuck in the butter
dish. He didn't wake when I moved the tray, or when I
removed the extra pillow and lay his head back.

His face was transformed by sleep. The worry lines
in his forehead disappeared, and his tiredness seemed to

concentrate in the shadows under his eyes. His cheeks sagged, his lips parted slightly, and he breathed more slowly than anyone I've ever known. His eyes didn't move, so he must have been sleeping too deeply to be dreaming.

I decided to sketch him, so I got my drawing pad and charcoal, and drew a half-dozen pictures. I sat in a chair beside the bed for all but the last one, which I did sitting beside him. That's when I realized how handsome he might be if he were to shave, brush his hair, get a little sun and put on a few pounds.

His eyes are very dark and deep-set, wolflike, but his lips are full and soft. Since he smiles or is about to smile almost constantly, I didn't see the wolf in him until he was asleep.

Mother says he's a good man, tortured by his past, running from his future. She came in while I was sketching him and read his palm. She said he had, or would have, two children, three wives, and that he was an artist trapped in the body of a scientist.

We acted childishly, I know, but after three weeks of being cloistered with George, we were both ecstatic to have a visitor. Neither of us could wait for him to wake up to begin our investigations.

7.

After breakfast the next morning, Helen convinced Louie to avail himself of George's spare wheelchair and to join them for a stroll and roll along the boardwalk. It was a lovely day, the dark blue sky dotted with cotton-ball clouds. The dog led the way, Helen pushed George, Andrea pushed Louie, and Helen did most of the talking. They went south until they encountered stairs, then they rolled out to the edge of the dunes and had a look at the rain-swollen Pajaro River rushing into the sea.

"When we first came here," Helen said, shouting to

be heard over the waves, "there was only one house on the dunes, and the developers still hadn't received final permission to subdivide, but we put a deposit down anyway and crossed our fingers." She sighed and patted George's shoulders. "I see now, with all the houses here, what a mistake this was, ecologically, I mean, but at the time we couldn't bear the thought of not living here if that were possible."

"If not you, someone else," said Louie, reaching down to touch the sand. "Besides, the dunes will be here long after these houses have turned to dust."

"Now that's reassuring," said Helen, tilting her head to think about it. "Except it implies that there won't be any *re*building, which I would imagine there will be, barring a nuclear war or a basic change in human values, which I suppose there might be, what with us running out of everything." She gave her husband a quick kiss. "I do wish you could join in, George. This is one of your favorite topics."

"Which values would have to change?" asked Andrea, taking the stick from Buka's mouth and throwing it down onto the beach below.

"The valuing of things," said Louie, without pausing to think.

"I didn't say human *nature*," said Helen, shaking her head. "Values exist to control human nature, which seems to be fairly unalterable. It is our nature to want things, and if you'll pardon my philosophizing, it is Nature that will teach us the limits of what we can have."

"Or how much more violent we have to be to get what we want," said Louie, looking out to sea. "Nature doesn't say 'Go easy.' Nature says 'Run, hide, kill, or be killed.' "

40

"Dad's getting cold," said Andrea, turning Louie around. "Let's go home."

"Shouting over the waves," said Helen, turning George around, too. "Demosthenes learned to speak by putting pebbles in his mouth and shouting over the waves."

"Maybe that's what I oughta do," said Louie, mumbling to himself.

Helen didn't hear him, but Andrea did, and to let him know she had, she put her hands on his shoulders and squeezed him gently.

"But George insists that's just a myth," said Helen, pushing ahead quickly. "Because when he tried it, he nearly broke a tooth, didn't you?" She waited the appropriate amount of time for a reply, then turned back to Louie and said, "I have this fantasy that he's remembering all my stupid questions, and one night he's going to wake up and inundate me with answers."

Helen

I don't put much stock in palm reading, except when my guesses turn out to be true. I depend more on how people respond to certain things I say. George calls them my litmus lines. One of them is, "Life just isn't fair." Most people will readily agree. Most very wealthy people will emphatically disagree. The academically oriented like to argue the definition of *fair*. Louie thought about it a moment, started to say something, then stopped himself and shrugged. I liked that.

I look into Louie's eyes and I see myself when I was

42

young. I see his great indecisiveness, his fear of death, his bridled lust. I see him watching Andrea and I get chills thinking about them making love. I think they would devour each other.

I would like to know more about him, but he has a way of deflecting my questions so that I end up doing all the talking. I've determined that he is both drawn to and repelled by the town of Santa Cruz. He said he's been circling around it for several months now, trying to get up the courage to go back there and face some old foes.

So at lunch, without really thinking, I called him a knight errant. He gave me the oddest look and said that's exactly how he felt about himself, only with an emphasis on the word *errant*. Andrea asked him what his error had been, and he said, without hesitation, "To let others act for me."

We then played a game of Scrabble, a minute per move, and I had him badly beaten until the very end when he spelled the word *index,* with the *x* on a triple letter and the whole thing on a triple word, *and* the *x* beside an *o* in the adjoining word, so that he scored hundreds of points, won the game, and left me wondering if he'd just been toying with us the whole time. Then he went to bed and Andrea took the dog for a run.

George was asleep and there was nothing to do, so I started a fire, got down a volume of Robert Graves and read a few love poems that put me right to sleep. I had a dream, just a brief scene, really, where George was very young, and he was chasing me through a dark forest. I wanted him to catch me, so I didn't run very fast, and I think, right before I woke up, he caught me.

8.

It was the afternoon of his second day in the house on Pajaro Dunes. Louie was sitting up in bed, trying to write a letter to his parents. He heard Andrea come in the front door with Buka. As he listened to the sounds of her filling the dog's bowl with water, he absentmindedly turned to a fresh page in his notebook.

He wrote her name in big block letters, ANDREA, then he drew vines and flowers and birds all around the letters. On the adjoining page, he wrote her name backwards, and his name backwards beside it:

AERDNA and EIOUL

Beneath the names, he wrote:

And Zeus, lonely in his absence from Olympus, turned a wild olive into a woman, mated with her, then flew away. The woman bore twins, Aerdna and Eiuol, though they were not siblings, but of opposite blood. When they were grown, they mated, giving birth to many children of such splendid beauty that . . .

There was a light knock at the door. Louie stopped writing, capped his pen and closed his notebook. "I'm awake," he said.

The door opened and Andrea leaned in. She was wearing a headband, a sweatshirt, and red University of Virginia gym shorts, which gave Louie his first look at her lovely legs. Her face was flushed and she was smiling radiantly. "Hello," she said, "are you busy?"

"Terribly," said Louie, frowning at her, "what with the merger pending and the crisis in Washington."

"Don't laugh," she said, coming into the room. "Dad used to make business deals in bed."

"Oh yeah?" said Louie, bouncing his eyebrows like Groucho Marx. "What business was he in?"

"He built factories," she said, sitting at the foot of the bed. "First, he invented part of a computer, then he started manufacturing the part, and then he built the factories where the computers were manufactured. And then he retired and had a stroke." She put her hands on her knees and leaned forward. "Anyway, I was running and decided I wanted to get to know you, and that it was silly for me to pretend I didn't, so I decided to just come in here and talk to you."

"Oh," Louie said, tapping his notebook with his pen. "Well, here I am."

"Or maybe I want to explain myself to you. I'm not sure why." She frowned at him. "Is that a common occurrence? I mean, do lots of people confide in you?"

"People seem to trust me," said Louie. "I'm not sure why."

"You don't seem to want anything," she said, clasping her hands around her knee and rocking back. "Maybe that's it."

"*Seem* is the key word there," said Louie, opening his notebook. He uncapped the pen and began to doodle. "I want all sorts of things. It's just that as long as I keep living like this, it's sort of enforced deprivation." He smiled down at his doodles. "But after three years on the road, I feel like it's time to get off."

"You make it sound like an addiction," she said, frowning at him.

"It is," he said, nodding. "Once your body gets used to it, you can pretty much stop thinking about anything but moving. You just go, and getting somewhere is just part of going, and everything blends together. Time stops meaning anything. There's no such thing as late or early. There's just cold and hot, wet and dry, hungry and not so hungry."

"What about people?" she asked, almost whispering.

"There aren't any people. There are fellow phantoms and female phantoms and phantoms in your dreams. But they never get a chance to become real because you never stay long enough. You only stay in one place when you're alone."

"You've been here two days," she said, arching her eyebrows.

"I know," he said, looking at her. "I better watch out." Then he smiled and said, "You were going to explain yourself."

She got up from the bed and sat in the chair. She

46

crossed her legs, then uncrossed them and put her hands on her knees again. "I don't know why it matters, but for some reason I want you to see me as a grown-up, a college professor. I feel like you see me as this rich girl, stuck with her parents." She shrugged. "I guess it doesn't matter. I promised my mother a long time ago that if he ever got sick, I would come and stay until he got better or died. But he's not going to get better, and he may not die for a long time."

"You could take them back to Virginia with you, couldn't you?"

"Mother won't leave. She says something is going to happen soon." Andrea stood up and walked around the bed to the window. She rested the palms of her hands on the sill and looked out at the dunes. "My mother and father," she murmured, and then her voice trailed off and she turned back to look at Louie. Her face was pale, her eyes moist, as if she might cry. "My mother doesn't do things like other people. She's not going to let George just vegetate. They made a pact a long time ago that if something like this happened to one of them, the other would do something to help them die."

Louie nodded. "I remember thinking the same thing when I used to go visit my grandmother. I told my sister, if I ever get that way, just stop feeding me."

"It's hard," she said, leaving the window and sitting on the bed again. "It's one thing to say it, and another to do it. To know *what* to do."

"So she's getting up the courage?" asked Louie.

"She's got that. I think a part of her still hopes he might recover."

"He might," said Louie. "You never know."

"Oh, I think we know he won't," she said, toying with the blanket. "We just don't want to believe it."

"You know what?" said Louie, reaching out and

taking her hand. "I'd love a beer, and you should have one, too."

"We don't have any beer," she said, quickly standing up, taking her hand away. "But I have to go to the store anyway, so what kind would you like?"

"Dark and bitter," he said, smiling at her. "But I'm easy. Anything is fine."

Marie

Louie rented an apartment in Soledad when I went into prison there. He said it was for Billy and the kids to have a place to stay when they came to visit, but I think he was planning to stay there until I got out. Then something must have happened, because he disappeared.

I still write to his parents every month, but they don't know where he is either. It wasn't until last year we even knew he was alive. A friend of Billy's saw him playing piano in a pizza parlor in San Luis Obispo. The guy said Louie looked emaciated, and when he tried to talk to him, Louie picked up his backpack and walked out of the place.

It's hard for me to think of Louie as skinny. He was so muscular and broad-shouldered, solid. I remember once when we were dancing, he picked me up and held me in the air for the longest time, and it didn't tire him at all. That was the night we almost went to bed. I never should have let the chance go by. But there was something so damn noble about him, I couldn't stick to my instincts.

When I told the prison psychologist about him, she said he sounded like a classic manipulator. She said we were having an affair, whether he slept with me or not. She said he was using me, not risking anything, because talk is cheap and Louie was a great talker. He used me as a way to stay away from home, so he wouldn't have to face what a mess his life was. She said I was his emotional babysitter and that he never really loved me.

That's when I tried to hate him, but I couldn't. It's never as simple as they say it is, and people aren't ever just one thing or another. I could see that Louie had used me, but I used him, too. People don't just sit around *being* with each other, they *get* from each other, or what's the point? I know he loved me and I know besides wanting him, I loved him, too. It didn't matter how my life changed, how bad or good things got, I still dreamt about him, dreamt about us being together.

9.

Louie sat out on the deck, his eyes closed, his shirt off, his feet up on the rail. The sun warmed his eyelids and sweat rolled down his face. Helen slid open the glass door and came out to chat. She was wearing one of George's sweaters with the sleeves rolled up.

"You are so skinny," she said, looking at Louie and shaking her head disapprovingly. "Have you always been?"

"No," he said, squinting up at her, "my ribs used to be invisible."

"George is skinny now, too," she said, pursing her lips and frowning. "For the last twenty years he's been trying to lose his tummy, but never could. Now he has and he probably can't even appreciate it."

"Maybe he can," said Louie, shading his eyes.

"I doubt it," she said, leaning on the rail and looking out to sea. "We used to communicate extrasensorily, you know."

"You actually had conversations?"

"Yes," she said, rubbing her throat as she breathed deeply. "Now I can't get anything. Oh, I know when he's hungry, when he wants his pipe. I hear the primal things still, but we used to share such great thoughts, such complexities." She turned and faced Louie, her eyes sparkling. "We went beyond language, you see. It was like an exchange of light!"

"Did you feel it or see it?" asked Louie.

She sat in the chair beside him. "It wasn't like feeling *or* seeing. It was as if the walls of our minds had given way, and the nerve endings, somehow, through invisible filaments, had become connected. We'd even have the same dreams. We'd wake up and talk about them as if we'd both just seen the same motion picture." She gave Louie a cautionary glance. "There were nightmares, too."

"And were you one person in those dreams?"

"One and the same," she said, bewildered. "How did you know to ask?"

"What did you look like?" he said, taking his feet off the rail and sitting up.

Andrea came out onto the deck. "Excuse me," she said, sounding very tired. "Aunt Becky's on the phone. I don't think she's coming."

"Damn!" said Helen, getting up and hurrying inside.

52

Andrea took her mother's seat, shaded her eyes and sneered at the ocean. "I wish the wind would stop for five minutes. It drives me crazy sometimes. It's incessant."

"Can't have dunes without the wind," said Louie, leaning back in his seat. "Your mother was just telling me about . . ."

"I know," said Andrea, glaring at him. "Her extrasensory powers."

"Did you overhear or are you clairvoyant, too?"

She put her feet up on the rail beside his and rocked back in her chair. "I overheard," she said, clasping her hands together tightly. "I've only had one clairvoyant experience in my life and it was awful. I haven't gone out of my way to have another one."

"I'd like to hear about it," Louie said, quietly. "I'm fascinated by things like that."

"I was fifteen. That was eighteen years ago." She shook her head and sighed. "Now you know how old I am."

"Let's see," he said, counting on his fingers, "fifteen plus eighteen is . . ."

She ignored him. "I was fifteen and we were living in Boston, and I was upstairs doing my algebra, minding my own business." She stopped and gave him a disparaging look. "Are you sure you want to hear this?"

"Yes," he said, "but not if you don't want to tell me."

"I'm just in a bad mood," she said, bumping his feet with hers. "Anyway, suddenly, in my mind, I saw my father making love to a woman, a friend of ours. And it was particularly shocking because I'd never seen anyone making love. I tried to shake the vision away, but it just kept being there. I shut my eyes and put my hands over my ears and hummed, you know, how kids do, but it didn't do any good. Then the woman got out of bed and they did it standing up, against the wall. And it turned out it was really happening, right at that moment."

"Are you sure?" he asked, doubtfully.

"Of course I'm sure!" she snapped, taking her feet down from the railing. "He was having an affair with her!"

"I mean," said Louie, putting a hand on her shoulder, "are you sure you really saw it and didn't just create the vision because you knew about it?"

"But I *didn't* know about it," she said fiercely. "I *couldn't* have known about it."

"It's funny you should say that," said Louie, his voice shaky, "because my wife, when she was my wife, was sleeping with other men all the time, and everybody knew about it but me. Except I must have known. I *had* to have known. But I wanted so badly for it not to be true, I wouldn't let it become a conscious thought. I'm just saying, maybe that's what you did."

"Where is she now?" Andrea asked, unclasping her hands and standing up.

"I have no idea."

"I was married once," she said, moving to the door. "When I was nineteen until I was twenty-three." She shook her head slowly. "What a stupid waste of time."

"Don't be so hard on yourself," Louie said, reaching out and pulling the empty chair over beside his. "Why do you always get up and leave right when we're getting to the interesting stuff?"

"I have to make lunch," she said, sliding the door open.

"I won't hurt you," he said, patting the seat of the chair.

54

"I'm not so sure about that," she said, going in. Then she came back out. "What I mean is, I'm not sure I want you to know me very well."

"I know what you mean," he said, taking his feet down from the rail. "Because if I *know* you, I'll be able to hurt you, right?"

"I like you," she said, smiling sadly. "When you leave tomorrow or the next day, it would be nice to still like you."

"Lunch," said Louie, winking at her, "sounds like a terrific idea."

Helen

We are both drawn to him, but for her the sexual pull is there, and it must be hard to separate it from the fascination about who he is and why he is a lost soul.

Andrea has had a calm, convenient relationship with a man in Virginia for the past year. She's even spoken of marriage, but always in such exhausted tones, as if she's settling for Frank because it's *time* to settle, not because she loves him. I've met the man, and he's very nice, but in that maddeningly complacent way that so many middle-aged professionals have. He looks right, he says the right things, but there's nothing surprising about him. Even his ideas are predictable, and that, for me, is the ultimate disappointment.

But when I consider how many men Andrea has known, just the ones *I've* heard of, I imagine she's grown weary of the search. I married George when I was seventeen and he is the only man I've ever slept with, where Andrea has had dozens of lovers, but has never found that truly compatible soul, which I found on my very first try. I think that's what frightens her about Louie. For all his external deficiencies, he seems to be a good match for her. I'm not saying he's the one. After all, we hardly know him. He might be the very opposite of what he seems. But he points up the possibilities that simply aren't there with Frank.

His senses are so highly tuned, where Frank seems to let most of the nuances of life just float by. Louie notices things. He hears every word, every sound, every subtle shift in tone. He is a receptor, wide open to the data we supply him, and he takes it all in with such empathy, with so little need to judge. Andrea has tried, I've heard her, to lead him into arguments, to expose his anger and impatience, but he remains unperturbed. He seems to have freed himself, to a great extent, of the need to prove anything.

And yet he hovers between the past and the present, waiting, as I am waiting, for the right moment to act. For him, it will be a going back, a confrontation with his past. For me, it will be a going forward, to a point of departure, to a launching of my husband's body.

10.

They ate avocado sandwiches and mushroom soup in the dining nook. The wind blew fiercely outside, tousling the dune grass and spraying the windows with sand. George sat at the table in his wheelchair. Helen sat beside him, feeding him spoonfuls of yogurt. Andrea sipped at her wine and frowned out at the dunes. Louie, aware of a growing tension in the air, concentrated on his food.

Helen wiped the yogurt from George's lips, then put the pipe in his mouth, but he pushed at it with his tongue and it fell, clattering on the floor. "Damn!" said

Helen, glaring at George as she knelt to pick up the pipe. "You see the mess it makes? You see what a filthy habit it is? I wish you'd quit!"

"Mother," said Andrea, softly cajoling, "he doesn't understand."

"Don't 'Mother' me!" said Helen, shaking the pipe at her. "You encourage him. You're always refilling it for him."

"You're tired," said Andrea. "You need to rest."

"The only thing I'm tired of is cleaning up his messes!" she said, dropping the pipe in George's lap. Then she gave Louie a fierce look and left the room.

Andrea sat very still, staring at her soup, then she pushed away from the table and got up to go after Helen. "I'm sorry," she said, without looking at Louie.

George remained immobile, save for a slight quivering in his eyes. The corners of his mouth turned down slightly, so he seemed regretful, but that was how he always looked. His hands lay inert in his lap, one on either side of the accursed pipe.

"Must be tough," said Louie, speaking to George. "I guess the pipe is her way of making you seem more alive."

A few minutes later, Helen came back into the kitchen. She'd changed from her slacks into a long skirt. She was carrying her coat and a small suitcase. "George," she began, her eyes moist, "I'm going to Carmel, to Becky's. I have to get away, dear." She leaned over and kissed George on the forehead, then turned to Louie. "Andrea's driving me. She'll be back in a few hours." Helen glanced furtively at her husand, then looked away. "You might want to refill his pipe for him. When you put it in his mouth, put it on the left side. Your left, his right. He has better grip there."

"I'll take good care of him," said Louie, getting up.

"I know," said Helen, turning away. "We trust you."

When the women were gone, Louie wheeled George out onto the deck. "Nice ocean," he said, checking to see if George's pipe was still lit. Buka scratched at the glass and Louie let him out. The dog ran down the steps and disappeared into the dunes.

"I'm going to try some ESP," he said, sitting in a chair beside George. "Try to make your mind completely blank, if it isn't already."

He held one of George's hands and looked out to sea, focusing on the horizon. The smoke drifted up from George's pipe, the clouds over the bay took on a pinkish tinge, and the gulls struggled northward against the wind. Louie closed his eyes and settled back in his chair. After a few minutes, he opened his eyes and looked at George. There was no visible change in the man's countenance. "I'll bet you want to fly away," said Louie, smiling sadly. "I don't blame you."

The pipe had gone out, so Louie packed in some fresh tobacco and relit it. He took a few puffs to get it going, then wedged it back in George's mouth.

"So anyway," said Louie, putting his feet up on the railing, "I took mescaline once, in Arizona, and I had a very powerful reaction to it. I thought I met this person, this very strange dark man, who said he was the mortal we often mistook for God. I was in no position to argue with him, and he knew some pretty good tricks."

Louie laughed self-consciously. He stood up and began to massage George's shoulders. "Anyway, this person, whoever he was, said that eventually the human race would evolve into hermaphrodites and would communicate extrasensorily. I asked him about sex and he showed me this image in the air, like a hologram, of two people making love, both penetrating, both receiv-

60

ing. But the thing was, their heads were connected, too, by these long translucent tubes with light shooting through them, which is sort of how Helen said it was for you guys."

Louie waited a few moments, then said, "It must be tough to go from that to this."

Andrea

I was just starting back from Carmel, when I realized that I was going to be alone with Louie. Mother and I had had a giggly, nervous conversation on the way to Becky's about leaving Louie alone in our house with George, but we hadn't gone beyond the joke that there wasn't much he could do to father, and there wasn't much to steal. But the fact was, I was going home, and I would be alone with a man I barely knew, though that wasn't what frightened me. I trusted Louie. What I didn't trust was my attraction to him.

I drove into Monterey and spent an hour in a bookstore, but everything I picked up was about sex. When I fled to the oversized art books, every print seemed to be of lovers.

I knew I wanted to make love with him, but I was so sure it would end sadly, no matter how nice it might be, that I hoped he would be gone when I got home. Then I could mourn a lost chance instead of resenting another brief sexual encounter. Not that there's anything wrong with brief sexual encounters. But they work best when they're just that, and not the culmination of falling in love.

11.

Louie stood at the kitchen counter, putting full weight on his wounded leg for the first time. He was brewing tea for himself and bouillon for George. He heard the front door open, picked up the two mugs and walked slowly into the living room. Andrea was standing in the doorway, apparently in no hurry to come in from the cold.

"Hello," said Louie, setting the mugs down on the coffee table.

"You shaved," said Andrea, stepping inside and closing the door behind her. She looked at him as if she couldn't believe what he'd done.

64

"Good or bad?" said Louie, touching his cheek.

"A definite improvement," she said, going past him into the kitchen. "Is there more hot water?"

"Yes, and I made some coffee, too," said Louie, following her.

"How's George?" she asked, pouring herself a cup and moving quickly into the living room.

"Fine," he said, turning to watch her. "I gave him a bath. He seemed to enjoy it."

"You bathed him?" she asked, putting a hand on her father's shoulder. She continued to look at Louie as if he'd grown a third eye.

"Well, see," said Louie, "I was taking a bath with my leg propped up so it wouldn't get wet, and the warm water felt so good, I thought it'd be nice if he had one, too. I'm pretty sure he liked it."

"How could you tell?"

"He kind of gurgled and splashed a little."

"That was nice of you," she said, trying not to cry.

"Well, you've been so nice to me."

"Have you eaten?" she asked, turning to look at the fire.

"I was waiting for you," he said, shoving his hands in his pockets.

"I'll fix something," she said, moving toward him.

"I already fixed it," he said, glancing back at the stove. "It'll be ready in ten minutes. I hope you like chile rellenos."

They were about to eat, when Buka ran up onto the deck and scratched at the glass, eager to come in and see Andrea. Louie slid open the door and the dog darted in, bringing with him a powerful odor of death.

"Phew," said Louie, wrinkling his nose and backing away.

Andrea shook her head, grabbed Buka by the collar

and dragged him back out onto the deck. "Stay," she said, shaking a finger at the dog. Then she closed the door and joined Louie at the table. "He loves to roll in dead things," she said, sitting down and unfurling her napkin. "This looks wonderful."

"I hope it's good," he said, chewing nervously on his lower lip. "I haven't cooked anything like this in a long time."

"It's delicious," she said, savoring her first bite. "I'm impressed. I wish mother were here."

"I kind of wanted to leave before she gets back," said Louie, starting to eat. "I'm terrible at saying goodbye. My leg's pretty much healed, and I've already stayed too long."

"Where will you go?" she asked.

"I don't know. South, maybe. It's warmer."

"It's warm here," she said, stabbing at her food. "You're not in the way, and you really should give the leg a few more days, and besides, mother would be heartbroken if you left, and I just don't think you should go yet."

"She'd be upset?"

"Yes," said Andrea. "She likes you very much."

After dinner, after they'd put George to bed, Andrea bathed Buka. Louie made a feeble attempt to sit by the fire and read, then he sauntered down the hall and stood in the bathroom doorway, watching Andrea scrub the dog.

"I have to take him to a party tomorrow night," she said, kneeling beside the tub, energetically shampooing Buka's golden hair.

The dog loved the bath. His eyes were wide with pleasure. When Andrea dipped the pitcher and poured water over him, he barked appreciatively and tried to shake himself dry. Andrea was wearing shorts and an old T-shirt to do the job, and she was as wet as the dog by the end of the bath.

Louie handed her a towel and she draped it over Buka, then lifted him out of the tub. Together, she and Louie dried the dog. When they released him, he shook himself and trotted out of the bathroom.

Then, before Louie could leave, Andrea stood up and closed the door. The bathroom was warm and steamy from the dog's bath. Andrea put her arms around Louie and kissed him, tonguing his mouth open. Then she backed away, took off her shirt, slipped off her shorts and moved close, kissing him again.

"I want to see you," she said, unbuttoning his pants. In a single swift movement he pulled off his T-shirt, while she carefully guided his pants down over his wound. She took his cock in both hands and brought it into her mouth. He reached down and gently held her head as she sucked on him. Then she got up, stood on her tiptoes and lowered herself onto him, closing her eyes as he entered her. "Louie," she said softly, clutching his shoulders.

"Yeah," he said, grimacing, "except my leg . . ."

"Oh God, I'm sorry," she said, lifting herself off him.

"Maybe if we tried it lying down," he said, opening the door and limping out into the hall. "I've heard of people doing that."

"No jokes," she said, taking his hand and leading him to her bedroom.

"This is pretty sudden," he said, hesitating.

"No it's not," she said, letting go of his hand to pull back the covers on the bed.

"I have to warn you, I think I'm in love with you," he said, carefully getting into bed beside her.

"No you're not," she said, tensing. "You don't

have to say that. You don't have to say anything. It doesn't matter."

"Yes, it does," he said, touching her cheek, caressing her. "It frightens me to love you."

"Don't be afraid," she said, taking him firmly by the shoulders and pulling him on top of her.

"I love you," he said, looking at her in amazement.

"Good," she said, hooking her legs around him, pressing her heels into his back. "Good."

Marie

When I was twelve and just starting to get boobs, my mother started telling me about sex and love. Sex was simple, she said, and love was hard, and putting the two together was almost impossible.

One night we were sitting in the kitchen, huddled around the woodstove, wondering if we'd ever see my daddy again, when my mother told me, "Never say 'I love you' to a man unless you want to lose him, marry him, or wreck him. Because when you say it, they'll either run, fall at your feet, or just plain fall apart. The ones that leave, well, good riddance, but be careful about the ones that stay. They won't ever leave you alone once you've said those words, so you'd better be damn sure you want them around all the time before you say it.

"And watch out when they say it to you, because if you like them at all, and they catch you off guard, they'll get you. You won't really *want* to love them, but once you let yourself *think* you love somebody, then you do, even if you know that besides being in love, you don't really like them."

She was trying to explain why she married my father, and she was trying to save me from a similar fate. But here I am, fifteen years later, drinking my wine, staying up late, wondering where Louie is, wondering if I ever told him I loved him. He said it to me, I know that, but I'm not sure I ever said the words to him. I know it wouldn't have made any difference, but it's the kind of thing I think about when I can't sleep.

12.

Louie stood behind Andrea, his arms around her waist, while she peeked under the pancakes to see if they were done. He rested his chin on her shoulder and closed his eyes. She could feel him growing heavier. "Hey," she said, pushing back against him, "you can sleep after breakfast."

"I am groggy from love," he said, standing up. "Who are you really?"

"You must have put something in the rellenos," she said, stacking the pancakes on a plate. "Ready?"

"Ready," said Louie, and they moved as one, stepping in unison like vaudevillians.

"Are we going to eat standing up?" she asked, setting the plate on the table in the dining nook.

"No," he said, kissing her neck, "you can sit on my lap."

"Is this perpetual contact absolutely necessary?"

"You don't like it?"

"I like it," said Andrea, "but it makes movement difficult."

"That's the idea," said Louie, sliding his hands up so they cupped her breasts. "I don't want to stop touching you."

"I appreciate that," she said, turning in his arms and kissing him. "I don't want to stop touching you, either. But I need to step back sometimes to look at you. When you're so close, I can't see you."

"I really am afraid to let you go, you know? I've never felt like this before."

"Well, I have, lots of times," said Andrea, shrugging. "You'll get used to it."

Louie released her. "Is that true? Have you really felt like this before?"

"Not *just* like this," she said, "but close."

"God," said Louie, shaking his head, "there goes another illusion."

"And you?" she said, seriously.

"Nothing even close," he said, sitting down. "It's amazing. I never thought I could make love so many times in one night."

"Oh, *that?*" said Andrea, pouring his coffee. "That is rather unusual, even for me. But let's not confuse sexual compatibility with love."

"Oh, let's," said Louie, closing his eyes and smiling sublimely.

"And then you'll leave, right?" said Andrea, her jaw trembling, tears filling her eyes.

"No," said Louie, taking her hand and pulling her onto his lap. "You've convinced me to stay."

After breakfast they carried George down to the beach and laid him on a blanket beside a driftwood log that shaded him from the sun and sheltered him from the wind. They threw sticks for Buka, played a little Frisbee, hugged and kissed, and began to build a sand castle.

Two young boys riding sting-ray bikes on the hardpacked sand stopped to help Louie and Andrea create the mound of sand from which the castle would be crafted. A few minutes later their father arrived with two shovels. He had been watching them through binoculars from their beach house. Before long, the work force included several more children, two teenagers, and three adults, all of them eagerly following Louie's orders.

The castle, completed after several hours of work, had high sloping walls, innumerable turrets and archways, a secret inner chamber, a moat and a driftwood flagpole, from which Andrea's blue bandanna fluttered. The adults ran off to their houses and beach blankets to get their cameras, while the children continued to work furiously, building a great sea wall to protect the fortress from the rising tide.

Andrea put her arm around Louie and pressed close to him. "It's beautiful," she said softly. "You're more than an architect, you're an artist."

"I'm a piano player," said Louie, shrugging. "This is nothing more than a barely modified version of Count Bragoni's castle at Elsinore."

"Bullshit," said Andrea, her southern accent thickening. "That there's original."

The photo session over, the kids took control of the castle and declared war on the incoming waves. Within

73

the hour, however, despite the children's heroic efforts, the walls and turrets had vanished back into the flat expanse of sand, as if they had never existed.

Louie and Andrea carried George home, changed him, and put him to bed. Then they took a long hot shower together and made love in Louie's room, where they had a view of a brief, brilliant sunset.

Andrea

He can be so tender and then almost brutish, but never so that it frightens me. He seems to anticipate my desires, and I want to stop and say, "How did you know?" but I wait until after and then he says it's all me and he's just hanging on for dear life.

Then sometimes he'll lie there and tell me with his eyes that I should do anything I want to him, and I always want to, and I'm amazed again that he knows it's what I want to do at that moment.

And why, I wonder, haven't other men been like

this, and I think it's because they didn't see me, so much as they saw my body and how they could use it. Louie does that, too, but he synchronizes himself with me, so we end up playing off each other instead of taking turns. He watches my face, I watch his, and each time we know more and better.

13.

"Andrea?" said Louie, standing in the hallway and looking into George's room.

"What is it?" she asked, coming to him. She was wearing lipstick and a touch of eyeshadow for the party. With her frilly white blouse and bluejeans, and the way her hair was parted on one side, she appeared much too young to be teaching college.

"He seems to be focusing," said Louie, moving into the room and sitting on the bed beside George. "He seems to be listening."

"He gets like that sometimes," said Andrea, not wanting to see.

"Maybe we shouldn't leave him," said Louie, taking George's wrist and feeling his pulse. "It's faster than it was this afternoon."

"Listen," she said, running a hand through her hair, "we'll only be gone an hour or so. Mother will be home any minute now. She doesn't mind if we leave him, and he certainly doesn't."

"I know," said Louie, putting a hand on George's forehead, "but look at his eyes. I haven't seen that before. I think he's trying to move."

"He'll stop in a minute," she said, turning away.

"We'll be home soon," said Louie, whispering to George.

He turned off the light and went into the kitchen where Andrea was sitting, brushing her dog. "I feel funny in these clothes," he said, looking down at the slacks and shirt he'd found in George's closet.

"They are a little loose on you," said Andrea, smiling up at him. "But you look fine."

"Loose?" he said, touching his shirt. "Fancy is what they are."

"You look fine," she said, standing up and kissing him.

"So do you. Maybe we shouldn't go to this party. Maybe we should just walk around the house looking at each other."

"Unfortunately, Buka is the guest of honor," she said, clipping the leash onto the dog's collar. "We have to go."

They hurried along the boardwalk, stopping once to let the dog pee. It was a clear chilly night. A nearly full moon was lifting off the horizon as they climbed a long flight of steps to a house that resembled an enormous windmill.

"I don't know about this," said Louie, shoving his hands into his pockets.

"Don't worry," she said, ringing the doorbell, then taking Louie's arm. The door opened and Buka pulled them into the house. A man with a droopy mustache and bloodshot eyes greeted Andrea with a kiss on the cheek. He acknowledged Louie with a nod and beckoned for them to follow him into the living room, where the party was.

"I'll be right back," said Andrea, waving to Louie as Buka dragged her into the kitchen.

Louie stood still, letting his eyes grow accustomed to the dim light. Someone handed him a marijuana cigarette, but he passed it on without taking a hit. The music was loud and people were shouting to be heard. Then a woman approached him. He realized that he knew her, but couldn't remember her name. She was wearing a Guatemalan Indian blouse, leather pants and black high heels. Her hair was blond and frizzy. She was wearing so much makeup it was hard to tell what she really looked like.

"Louie?" she said, leaning toward him and squinting. "The piano player?" She laughed nervously. "Jesus, I heard you were dead. I was depressed for weeks. Jesus. You're not dead. My god, this is amazing." She moved closer and frowned. "You are Louie, aren't you? You sure look like Louie."

"I'm sorry," he said, nodding self-consciously, "I don't remember your name."

"Janet," she said, nodding with him. "A loyal fan. A Seaside Inn regular. I still am, but nobody plays like you guys did." She shook her head. "Wait until Maureen hears about this. She's the one who said you were dead."

"I'm not," said Louie, moving away slowly. "It was nice seeing you again. I have to go."

"Come by the inn some time," she said, waving to him. "Play for us."

Louie made his way into the kitchen, where two young Mexican women were preparing plates of deviled eggs and guacamole dip. He said buenas noches to them, and asked where the dog was. They both laughed and gestured that he should keep going. He passed through the kitchen into a wide hallway where he was confronted by three brightly colored doors. One of the doors was turquoise and had *Darkroom* written on it in flowing cursive script. Another of the doors was burgundy and had *Pissoir* scribbled on it in an imitation of graffiti. The third door was hot pink, dotted with hundreds of tiny red hearts. Louie could hear Buka yelping behind the pink door, so he opened it and went in.

It was large room, a photographic studio, with various colored backdrops propped against the walls. Andrea was standing in the center of the room, arguing with two women and the man with the droopy mustache. She was struggling to hold Buka. The poor dog was straining with all his might to pull away from her. At the far end of the room, a young female retriever was tied to the leg of a table. She was wagging her tail and waiting impatiently to be released.

"What's up?" asked Louie, sauntering over to the group.

"We're going," said Andrea, giving him a pained look. "Would you take Buka? He's breaking my arm."

Louie took the leash from her and knelt beside Buka, holding him around the chest with both hands. The dog continued to struggle, oblivious to everything but the female retriever.

"Now wait a minute," said the mustached man,

grimacing, "some of these people came all the way from San Francisco to see this."

"No!" said Andrea, pointing at him. "I don't care if they flew in from Paris. Either we leave the dogs alone or we forget it."

"Okay, we'll leave them alone," said the mustached man, rolling his eyes, "but I really think you're being unreasonable, babe."

Andrea glared at the floor and gritted her teeth. "And I'm going to stand at the door and make sure they're left alone."

"Okay, okay," said the man, holding his hands up in surrender. "We'll leave."

Andrea folded her arms and waited. The two women, sour with disappointment, trudged from the room. The mustached man untied the female dog and she skipped across the floor to Buka, then rolled onto her back submissively.

"Wow, she's ready," said the man, clapping his hands together and hurrying out of the room.

"That bastard," said Andrea, stamping her feet. "He *promised* me the dogs would be left alone."

"We can leave," said Louie standing up. "Buka will never forgive you, but . . ."

"No, we'll stay," she said, unclipping Buka's leash.

The love-hungry dog rushed over to a sky blue backdrop and peed on it. Then he approached the female, the hair on his chest and shoulders billowing like a lion's mane. Andrea and Louie left the room, closing the door quietly behind them.

The music in the living room died down and people began to hoot and cheer and applaud. The Mexican women picked up the plates of deviled eggs and hurried into the living room. The hooting and cheering grew louder for a moment, then suddenly died down.

"What in hell is going on?" asked Louie, leaning protectively against the door.

"I don't know," said Andrea, resting her head on his shoulder.

"I'll go see," he said, kissing her gently before leaving her. He walked through the kitchen into the living room and found everyone crowded around a four-foot-square television screen, mounted on the wall. On the screen, Buka was furiously humping the female retriever.

Andrea came up beside Louie, looked at the screen for a moment, then turned away. A moment later, the people began to boo as Andrea appeared on the screen and tried to separate Buka from the female. But the dogs were stuck together. This made the party-goers cheer. Andrea glanced around the room, discovered where the camera was hidden and walked toward it, her angry face filling the screen. When the screen went blank, someone said loudly, "What's wrong with that bitch?"

Louie turned and walked through the kitchen, placing himself in front of the door to the studio. The mustached man, followed by several people, approached him.

"Sorry," said Louie, folding his arms. "Private party."

"Come on," said the mustached man, rubbing his hands together nervously, "this *is* my house."

"The dogs don't care if we watch," said a woman, plaintively. "They don't care."

"Andrea cares," said Louie, smiling. "She's got her little quirks, and I've learned over the years to respect them or take the consequences." He sighed. "She can get pretty worked up."

A big man, his face twisted into a sneer, pushed close to Louie and said, "I think you better get outta the way so I can talk to her."

"No," said Louie, still smiling. "You don't understand."

"Forget it," said the mustached man, waving his hands. "Just forget it. It's not worth the hassle. I taped the best part already. We'll play it back."

"I wanted to see them finish," said another woman. "*That's* the best part."

"Forget it. It's not worth the hassle," said the mustached man, taking the big man by the arm. "I'll run it in slow motion. You'll love it."

When the people were gone, Louie opened the door and looked into the studio. Andrea was leaning against the wall, humming to herself. Her eyes were closed, her hands in her pockets. Buka whimpered as he finally managed to detach himself from the she-dog. He lay down, panting. The female walked slowly across the room, went under a table and lay down, too.

"They're done," said Louie, calling softly to Andrea.

She opened her eyes, blinked a few times, went to Buka and clipped the leash to his collar. "We can go out this way," she said, pulling her dog to his feet and dragging him to a side door.

The moon was so bright it startled them as they came out into the night. Louie took the leash from Andrea and held out his hand to her. She hesitated, but he kept holding his hand out until she took it.

Marie

I'm just about ready to go looking for him. I think about him more now than I did a year ago. Maybe that's because I've got everything I ever dreamt I'd get before I saw him again. Everything is ready now, and if I have to go get him I will.

My children need a man around, and Louie was so good with them, I can't help wanting it to be him. Cal is eight and Eva is six, and I guess I've been getting them ready for him, too. I'm so proud of how they're turning out. It just won't seem right until he sees them and talks to them and holds them again.

My brother, and the few friends I talk to about Louie, tell me as gently as they can that I'm crazy, that I'm setting myself up for a big disappointment. And there's nothing I can say to prove them wrong. It's just a feeling I have, that when he finally comes back, he will *have* to stay.

14.

When they got home the
wind was rushing through the house, the sliding glass
door was open, and George's bed was empty. Andrea
ran down the hall, calling her father's name. Louie
dashed out onto the deck, vaulted the railing and
crashed down through the dune grass to the beach.

He sprinted across the sand to the water's edge and
peered out at the frothy moonlit surf. He scanned the
first line of waves, then the second, and there was
George, standing naked in the trough of a giant wave,
his head bowed, as if he were praying. "Dive!" Louie
screamed, but it was too late. The wall of water fell on
top of the old man, and he vanished.

Louie pulled off his shoes and pants, then charged out into the surf. The salt water stung his wound, but the sea was so cold he was soon numb to any pain. He dove under a big breaker, then stood in water up to his waist and turned toward shore. Andrea and her dog were running south along the beach. She was pointing out at the waves.

Louie tried to walk through the water, but it was too rough, so he swam out another ten yards where he was able to catch the strong southward current. He let it pull him along until he came abreast of Andrea, then he fought the current, turning full circle twice before he spotted George, face down, swirling in the backwash of a wave. The old man's body was milky white in the moonlight, loose and floating like an enormous jellyfish.

Louie struggled through the choppy waters and grabbed George's arm. He tried to pull him shoreward, but the undertow was formidable. A massive breaker caught up to them and Louie threw his arms around the old man's waist and dove under the wave with him. They bobbed up amidst a chaos of smaller swells, Louie gasping for breath, struggling to keep George's head above the water. The current carried them south swiftly. Louie tried to shift his hold on the old man to a headlock, so he could more easily swim him into shore. When Louie's strength was almost exhausted, the waters around them grew relatively calm and he was able to get them in far enough to touch bottom.

Andrea waded out as far as she could and helped Louie carry her father up onto the sand, where they lay him on his back. She knelt beside him and tried to breathe life into him, but he was gone. She put her ear to his heart and began to cry. Louie stood above her, his teeth chattering, his body shaking with cold.

Helen

I arrived home moments after they brought his body into the house. I was shocked to find him dead, but more than that I was angry with him. He lay there on the couch, looking absurdly alive, his eyes refusing to stay shut, his body almost boyish in the half-light.

Louie hurried into the shower. Poor man was frozen to the bone. Andrea sat on the couch, crying, cradling George's head in her lap. I sat at his feet, took them into my hands and gave him a last massage.

He was biding his time, the old fox, knowing full

well we wouldn't let him go. Still, it hurt me that he'd had the wherewithal to escape like that, but hadn't wanted to communicate with me before going. I still had questions I wanted answered.

Louie came into the living room and put his hands on Andrea's shoulders and she leaned into his caress, so I knew they were lovers. I wondered if George had known, and for the moment before my sorrow overwhelmed me, I imagined that he had engineered everything.

He'd brought Andrea out to California with his stroke, somehow called Louie to Pajaro, then arranged the chance meeting, the wound, everything. It was absurd, I know, but it would have been just like George. And of course he'd want to test his hero with a rescue at sea, and if Louie hadn't gone out into the waves, I supposed George would have reluctantly returned to shore, a disappointed matchmaker.

Andrea and Louie sat with me, but after a while I sent them to bed. I said I wanted to be alone with George, which was true, but more than that I wanted to see if my intuition was correct, and by craning my neck, I could see them both going into Andrea's room. When they did, I was flooded with joy and jealousy.

I gave George a last kiss, then covered him with his favorite blanket, a tattered old woolly plaid thing he'd gotten from L. L. Bean a thousand years ago. Then I made myself some coffee, got out our will and read through it, seeing if there was anything I wanted to change. I added a paragraph giving Louie our rocking chair, which was silly, but I wanted to give him something.

15.

They were on their way to Watsonville to pick up George's ashes. They made small talk about the weather and the artichokes, and what a wonderful car the old Mercedes was. Then quite abruptly, Andrea asked Louie to come back to Virginia with her.

He stared out at the passing fields and tried to think of what to say. When he didn't reply, Andrea pulled over to the side of the road, shut off the engine and set the hand brake. Louie jumped out of the car, picked a bright yellow dandelion and handed it to her. She put it in her hair, then folded her arms and waited for him to say something. Louie saw a big patch of lupines not far down the road, so he went to pick them.

"This is very nice," said Andrea, as Louie deposited the enormous blue bouquet in her lap. "But what does it mean?"

Louie slumped in his seat, then sat up straight and cleared his throat. "I have to go to Santa Cruz," he said, grimly. "There's a woman there I have to say goodbye to, and I have to see my ex-wife and be done with all that. Then I'll get back to Virginia as fast as I can."

"Well," she said softly, "I have to kind of reorganize my life a little before you come out, anyway, and say goodbye to a few things myself."

They moved to each other and embraced, crushing flowers between them, filling the car with lupine perfume.

When they got to the crematorium, Andrea couldn't keep from crying. "I'm sorry," she said, wiping her eyes. "I'm sorry, could you go in, Louie?"

"Sure," he said, clicking on the radio and tuning it to a jazz station. "I'll be back in a minute."

The anteroom of the crematorium was dark and cool and odorless. Louie rang the service bell on the receptionist's desk, put his hands in his pockets and sat down to wait. There was a greenish painting of the ocean at sunset hanging on one wall. The other walls were covered with plaques, certificates and various photographic attempts at imitating Van Gogh's sunflowers.

A large, jovial woman with dyed red hair came hurrying out from behind the partition that separated the waiting room from the ovens. She was wearing a blue smock and her cheeks were shining from the heat.

"Thought I heard a bell," she said, removing her rubber gloves.

"I've come for George Arlen's ashes," said Louie, going to the desk.

"Just be a minute," she said pertly. "We're filling the urn right now." She handed Louie a small, neatly wrapped brown package. "These are his fillings," she said, tapping the box with her long fingernails. "Some places keep them, but with the price of gold being what it is, we don't think that would be fair."

"No," said Louie, "I guess it wouldn't."

On the way back to Pajaro, they stopped at a fallow field to gather mustard flowers, yellow and white, which they put in the trunk. Then they went to a liquor store and bought a small bottle of George's favorite cognac that Helen had requested. Once home, Louie carried the urn and the cognac, Andrea the flowers.

Helen was waiting in front of the house, her hair done in braids, tied with bright red ribbons. Buka was inside, scratching at the door, barking to be let out, but Helen didn't want him along to dispel the solemnity of the occasion. Louie led the way as they walked along the boardwalk, down the stairs and across the beach to the edge of the sea.

Andrea lay the mustard blooms down on the hard-packed sand where the last big wave had reached. Helen knelt and arranged the flowers in a circle, then motioned for Louie to pour the ashes into the center. He knelt beside her and shook out the gray flakes and chunks of bone. Helen spread them with her hands, then doused them with cognac and ignited them.

"We mustn't be afraid to be sentimental," she said, standing up, her knees wet.

"No," said Andrea, giving Louie a hand up.

"George, I loved you and I hated you," said Helen, speaking loudly to the ashes. "Sometimes, when you hurt me, I wished you were dead, and sometimes you brought me such joy I couldn't love you enough." She paused, her brow wrinkled, and then she smiled and her brow became smooth. "I miss you already, and I don't know how I'm going to measure things now, because I always measured them by you."

· Andrea took George's pipe out of her pocket and lay it atop the smoking ashes. "When I was little," she began, "you called me Andy. Wishful thinking. But for a long time I tried to be your boy. I tried to be Andy. But I just couldn't do it. I hope I haven't been too much of a disappointment to you. I'll miss you." She sighed and looked at Louie.

"Well," he said, quietly, "I didn't know him very well, but I liked him."

"Tell him," said Helen, taking Louie's hand. "Talk to him."

"I liked you," said Louie, speaking to the ashes. "I liked talking to you, looking at you."

Andrea took Louie's other hand and they stepped back a few paces. Andrea pointed to the horizon, and they moved back a few yards more. Moments later, a big wave rushed in and obliterated the ring of flowers, consumed the ashes and carried George's old pipe out to sea.

Andrea

I was able to keep my confusion and grief fairly well in check for most of the flight back to Virginia, but when we began our descent into Washington, D.C., I started to panic. California seemed an unreality again, along with everything that had just happened there.

I'd known Louie for ten days and I wanted him to move in with me. It seemed absurd and impossible. My analytical self took over. I saw my attraction to Louie as a denial of losing my father. Miserable woman, trapped in beach house with dying father and angry mother, seeks refuge in hallucinatory romance with charming derelict. Suddenly the thought of Louie coming back to Virginia was embarrassing to me. What would my friends say? What would my colleagues say? What would Frank say?

I rented a car and drove home from the airport, praying that Frank wasn't at my house, watering the indoor plants or feeding my cat. I stopped at a grocery store I'd never gone to before, to avoid seeing anyone I knew. When I got home, I snuck into the house like a thief. I stood in the kitchen, unable to imagine Louie being there with me, thinking I should call him immediately and tell him to forget it.

But I knew I wasn't in my right mind, so I ate something and strolled around the garden, seeing what had come up in my absence. I'd missed the beginning of spring, and I felt cheated. Most of my favorite tulips had come and gone already, only their long stems and a few dehydrated petals remained.

I went inside and wandered through the house and I began to relax, to feel connected again, to wonder what was going on at the university. I forgot, for a moment, that my father was dead, that my mother was in trouble, that I'd ever known anyone named Louie. I went to the phone to call my friend Patty, but I thought, no, she'll mention to Bob that I'm back, he'll say something to Frank, and I don't want Frank to know I'm back because I have to wait until I've gotten up the courage to tell him I'm in love with Louie.

Louie? Who is Louie? A man I met in California. He has a backpack and says he plays the piano, says he was an architect, and he really is quite intelligent and sensitive and a great lover, but beyond that, I don't know much about him, or if we'll be able to get along with each other in the real world, because he apparently doesn't feel capable of *being* in the real world.

But then I thought no, dammit, I'm not going to do this anymore. I'd been trying to *think* my way into love all my life, to properly match myself, to hold back my love until I was absolutely sure I'd made the right choice. I knew I could rationalize my way out of anything. What I had to do was shut off my brain for a moment and trust my heart.

So I called Pajaro to see how Mother was doing and to tell Louie I loved him. He wasn't there. Mother said she'd convinced him to borrow the car for his trip to Santa Cruz. He'd left right after he got back from taking me to the airport. She said he wanted to drive her out to Virginia. When I asked her if she would come, she laughed and said the trip might be just what she needed.

16.

When Louie exited off Highway One and followed Ocean Street to Water Street, Water to Pacific Avenue, he felt as if he were entering a time warp. He found a place to park behind the bookshop, looked at himself in the mirror and tried to smooth down his unruly hair. Then he got out of the car, locked up, took a deep breath and headed for the mall.

To the uninitiated, it might have seemed that some sort of spring celebration was taking place, but it was a normal day on the Santa Cruz mall. Young transients stood in groups, sharing cigarettes and booze, panhandling from the slower passersby. A man with a parrot on his shoulder pedaled by on a unicycle, while a Mexican woman with a patch over one eye tried to sell Louie an ounce of marijuana. Tourists mingled with colorfully garbed hippies. Street musicians filled the air with song. An old man wearing a blue beret, white slacks, and white patent leather tap shoes danced to a trio of saxophonists playing bebop, a mere ten yards from where an old man was rendering Christian hymns on a saw. Two people asked Louie where the post office was, and several others asked him to sign petitions. A tiny barechested man, with gray hair down to his waist, begged Louie for spare pennies.

There were Hare Krishna people banging cymbals, black men playing congas, and two fat men singing along with a cassette recording of German folk songs. There were jugglers and preachers, vendors and lunatics, and for every one doing something, there were six people watching, and for each person watching, there were six more hurrying by, though where they were hurrying was a mystery Louie had never solved.

He was just about to go into the bakery when someone tapped him on the shoulder. He turned around, expecting another panhandler, but was surprised to see a pretty young woman looking up at him, her mouth open in astonishment. It took him a moment to realize that it was the woman from under the bridge. Her hair had been cut extremely short and she was wearing a baggy white smock. She had a two-year-old child on her back and a sleeping infant strapped to her front. Holding out her hand expectantly, she asked, "Are you the guy who saved me?"

Louie nodded and she took hold of his wrist. "God," she said, urgently, "thank God they didn't kill you." She let go of his wrist and put her arms around him, pressing her cheek against his chest. Louie sucked in his stomach to keep from crushing the infant, while the child on the woman's back reached out and grabbed Louie's hair.

"I'm outnumbered again," said Louie, making a funny face at the child.

"Thank God," the woman said again, standing on her tiptoes to kiss Louie's cheek.

Louie waited for her to calm down, then stepped back from her and said, "My name is Louie."

"Oh, yeah," she said, laughing nervously. "I'm Chris." She turned her head and looked at the child on her back. "This is Ananda." Then she turned back to Louie and patted the baby she was carrying in front. "This is Mustafa Kahlil."

"They're very cute," said Louie, nodding.

"I can't believe you're really here," she said, taking his hand again. "Do you live around here?"

"No, I'm just passing through," said Louie, squeezing her hand and releasing it.

"Do you need a place to stay?" she asked, plaintively, taking his hand again. "At least let me fix you lunch. I live right near here. I really need to explain. Please?"

Louie hesitated, then moved with Chris out of the way of a roller skater. "Okay," he said, sighing. "I'll be there in an hour."

"Oh good," she said, going onto her toes to kiss him again. "It's 1225 Gharkey, number three, the big yellow house. I'm around back."

And then she was gone, as suddenly as she had appeared. Louie waited for a herd of crazy-looking people pushing shopping carts to pass by, then continued on his way. He dropped a dime in the jar on the

United Farm Workers' table, crossed to the shady side of the street and sat down beside the accordion player in front of Woolworth's.

"Hey, it's what's-his-name!" said the accordion player, a thin, sad-looking fellow with pale skin and a wispy goatee. "Haven't seen you in a long time. You lost weight. How've you been?"

"Okay. How are you?" asked Louie, dropping a quarter in the open accordion case.

"Still sittin' here," he said, smiling wryly. "Wanna play?"

"Okay," said Louie, turning sideways so he could get at the keys.

The accordion player pumped the bellows and pushed the chord buttons, while Louie played the keyboard two-handed. They did a Swiss-sounding "Saint Louis Blues" and attracted a small crowd. Several people threw quarters into the box, and afterward the accordion player offered to split what they'd made.

"No, I'm driving a Mercedes now," said Louie, rising to go.

"Take a buck," said the accordion player, rolling his eyes.

"It's not mine, but I'm driving it," said Louie, shrugging.

"There's no shame in being poor," said the accordion player, tugging at his goatee. "I'm poor, and I'm perfectly content."

"You ever get the urge to leave?" Louie asked him, simply.

"I live in paradise," said the accordion player, beginning a barcarole. "I'm happy."

Louie left the mall and walked north to Walnut Street, where he stopped in front of a beautifully renovated California bungalow, painted gray with black

100

trim. The sign hanging over the front porch said *Richardson, Alvarez and Goss, Architects.* Louie opened the gate and went up the walk to the front steps. He stood looking up at the sign for a moment, then went up the stairs two at a time.

The teen-age receptionist was filing her nails as Louie came in. She had a pouty expression on her face, but was otherwise quite pretty. Her modern teak desk, remarkably uncluttered, seemed out of place in the old house.

"Hi," said Louie, shoving his hands in his pockets. "Bob Goss in?"

"No," she said, putting her file down and picking up a pen. "Would you like to leave a message for him?"

"Yes," said Louie, looking around the room. "Tell him Louie Cameron dropped in to say hello."

She looked up, squinting curiously at him. "Louie Cameron?" she said, emphasizing the *Cam* in Cameron. "Who used to work here?"

"That's me," said Louie.

"Listen," she said, "I can probably catch Bob at the site."

"No, no. Don't bother," said Louie, shaking his head. "I just wanted to see the old place and say hi, that's all."

"He'll be disappointed he missed you," she said, scribbling Louie's name on the note pad. "They mention you all the time."

"I was a laugh a minute," said Louie, turning to go. "I used to design hilarious kitchens."

"Is there some way he can reach you?" she asked, calling after him.

"No," said Louie, pausing at the door. "Tell him I'm fine, and not to worry about me anymore."

101

Andrea

Frank brought me flowers. He'd lost some weight and looked much handsomer than I remembered him. He kissed me, called me sweetheart, told me how much he had missed me, how he'd searched his soul and decided he'd been a fool to ever withhold his love from me. He vowed that he was going to be the passionate lover he knew I'd always wanted him to be.

That was my cue to throw my arms around him, weep for joy and take him to bed. I thought of lying next to Louie, holding him in the warm aftermath of our loving. I decided it would be cruel to say to Frank that I'd found another, better lover. He didn't deserve that. Instead, I told him that, having had time to think, to sort out my feelings, I had decided to stop seeing him as a lover. I needed time to make some decisions about my life and career, and I was finding it impossible to do so in the context of our relationship as it had been.

All this was true. We'd talked about it before, many times. But this time it wasn't just talk, and he knew it. He began to cry. He begged me for another chance. I said it wasn't a question of chances, it was a question of being truthful to myself.

Frank wiped his eyes, regained his composure and apologized for being so emotional. I told him I loved his emotion. He forced a smile, looked at his watch, and said if I didn't mind, he would go.

I walked him out to his car and we embraced. I was feeling relieved and very much in control of the situation, when Frank grinned slyly at me and said, "You can't hide it from me, Andrea."

I asked him what he meant. He said that even he, a perceptual dullard, could see that I was in love with someone. He said he'd known it the moment he saw me. He had hoped the love radiating from me was for him. He said he was glad for me, and he thanked me for not saying anything about whoever it was.

I was about to tell him he was wrong, that I really *did* need to be alone, when he said that losing me to another lover was preferable to simply losing me. It freed him, where my saying I needed time to ponder the possibilities exiled him into limbo. He was, he said, too old for limbo.

17.

When Louie arrived at Chris's, she was standing at the stove, stirring vegetables in a wok. Ananda was playing with her blocks under the table. Mustafa Kahlil was asleep in his crib beside his mother's bed.

"Please have a seat," said Chris, taking a stack of folded diapers off a chair. "It's only one room, but it's cheap and I get sun almost all day."

"I thought you were much younger," said Louie, making sure not to kick Ananda's blocks.

"You didn't get a very good look that day," she said, filling two bowls with rice and vegetables.

104

She put the food in front of Louie, poured him a glass of white wine, then took a bag of groceries out of her daughter's highchair and set it on the floor. "Ananda, come and eat," she said gently.

The little girl crawled out from under the table and scaled the side of the chair unassisted. She smiled mischievously at Louie, put her hands in her mouth and burbled at him.

"Ever since Mustafa was born, she's been talking baby talk again," Chris said, sitting in the chair across from Louie.

"So," said Louie, raising his glass. "To your health."

"To yours," she said, clinking her glass against his. "I didn't get a chance to see how good-looking you were."

"Thanks," he said, sipping the wine. "Consider the debt repaid."

"You are," she said, her voice softening. "Not in a typical way, but you've got a very kind face."

"You're very kind to say so," he said, winking at her.

"Oh, God!" she said, startling Ananda.

"What?" said Louie, looking around the room.

"You're a Scorpio, aren't you?" she said, putting a hand on her heart.

"I think so," said Louie, relaxing. "I thought the place was on fire."

"Suddenly you were just being totally Scorpio," she said, her eyes wide.

"I winked," he said, nodding. "Do Scorpios do a lot of winking?"

"Well," she said, smiling knowingly, "*when* they wink, that's how they do it."

"I didn't used to believe in astrology," said Louie, bouncing his eyebrows at Ananda to make her smile.

"I'm very compatible with Scorpio men," said Chris, blushing slightly and giving Louie an inviting look. "I'm a Virgo, and my moon is in Taurus."

"I don't know where my moon is," said Louie, feigning sadness.

"I can do your chart," said Chris, eagerly. "Do you know the time of day you were born?"

"I know the time," said Louie, "but I can't remember the day."

"You're kidding?" she said, frowning at him.

"I'm kidding," he said, finishing his wine. "November seventh."

"Scorpio," she said, her smile returning. "See? You were just being totally Scorpio again."

After lunch, Ananda voluntarily took a nap. Mustafa Kahlil threatened to wake up, but then subsided. Louie cleared the table and was about to say goodbye, when Chris pulled him away from the sink and embraced him.

"I'll never forget what you did for me," she said, squeezing him. "I really think they were going to kill me." She shook her head and looked down at the floor. When she looked back up at him, her makeup was running down her cheeks. "You want to get loaded?" she asked. "It helps me talk."

Louie glanced at the door, then looked around the tiny room, his gaze settling on Ananda. She was asleep on her stomach, her thumb in her mouth, her little butt raised slightly. "You go ahead," he said, nodding. "I have to go soon."

Chris opened what appeared to be a closet door, revealing a toilet, above which hung some clothes. She lifted the top off the toilet tank, reached in and brought

106

out a plastic bag containing a Gerber's baby-food jar full of marijuana. "Can't be too careful," she said, taking out two prerolled cigarettes.

Louie sat down at the table and poured himself another glass of wine. Chris lit one of the joints and sucked deeply on it. She sat beside Louie, took another hit, then held the joint out to him. "Come on," she said. "It's nice stuff, it really is."

Louie looked at the joint and shook his head slowly, but as she began to take it away, he reached for it. He brought it close to his face and watched the smoke curl up from the joint tip. "I haven't done this for a couple years," he said quietly.

"How come?" she asked.

"Well, I like how it makes me feel, but then afterward I get real depressed. Sometimes for days."

"This is very mellow dope," she said, putting the unlit joint in her mouth. "I smoke it all the time and I don't get depressed. You keep that one."

Louie hesitated for a moment more, then put the joint in his mouth and began to smoke. Without thinking, they settled into a rhythm where one of them exhaled as the other inhaled. Louie noticed the pattern and smiled, realizing by his awareness of it that he was stoned. "That's very strong stuff," he said, looking deeply into Chris's eyes. "I have to go soon."

She took a final hit, then went to the sink and washed her face and hands. As she dried herself, she looked at Louie and said, "It just *seems* like I'm taking forever."

Louie nodded and grinned, then laughed at the thought of his grinning so enormously. He looked at Chris and was struck by how small she was, how minuscule her wrists were, how large her milk-swollen breasts were in proportion to the rest of her body.

"Well," she said, coming back to the table and sliding her chair close to his, "I needed to go to L.A., to see this guy who said he wanted to record a song I wrote." She smiled shyly at Louie and brought her feet up onto her chair. "I'll play it for you later maybe, but I didn't have any money, so I forgot about it until I ran into Ena, from my belly-dancing class, and she was with this guy Carl who was driving to L.A."

Louie sipped at his wine and drew circles on the tablecloth with his finger.

"Carl was weird," she said, nodding. "He looked like an accountant, you know, only he picked up hitchhikers. And pretty soon, the car was jammed with people and a dog, and he was driving all over, dropping people off and picking up other people, and I thought, 'Shit, I'll *never* get to L.A.,' but then Larry and Johnny were sitting there and they said they were going to L.A. and that I should come with them, because Carl was never going to get there."

Louie took off his sweater and smoothed back his hair. He wet his finger and ran it around the rim of the glass, trying to make the crystal sing. "You were in a hurry," he said, shaking his head.

"Yeah, and they said they knew a shortcut," she said, taking a sip of wine from Louie's glass. "So I went along because they seemed nice, you know, and then we got out of the truck and Larry thanked the guy and I should have known something was wrong because the guy gave me a weird look before he drove away and then they took me under the bridge."

"How can you say they were nice?" asked Louie, glancing incredulously at Chris. "They were rapists and they tried to kill me. How can you say they were nice?"

"Hey," said Chris, patting his hand, "don't get so

108

upset. They *seemed* okay." She laughed and shook her head. "I've been with lots worse, believe me."

"Why?" asked Louie, pushing away from the table. "It's sickening. Why would you?"

"Hey," she said again, "you just meet people. You don't *plan* it."

"That's crazy," said Louie, standing up. "I have to go."

"Oh, don't go," said Chris, reaching out to him. "I wanted to thank you."

"You did," said Louie, calming down.

"No, I mean really," she said, getting up and going to him.

She put her arms around his waist and pressed against him. He hugged her for a moment, then began to pull away but she held on, dropping her hands onto his buttocks and rubbing herself against him.

"No," said Louie, backing away.

"You're hard," she said, refusing to let go. "You want me."

"I *don't!*" shouted Louie, putting his hands on her shoulders and pushing her.

This forced her down so her face was pressed against his stomach. Keeping one arm around him, she began to unzip him. He took another step back, tripped over his chair, and together they crashed to the floor. Chris, undaunted, got her hand on Louie's cock and began to massage it. Louie pushed her hand away and tried to get up, but she had him pinned.

"You want it," she giggled, trying to pull his pants down. "I want it. We both want it."

"Please," said Louie, closing his eyes. "I think I hurt myself when I fell."

"You're okay," she said, straddling him. She lifted

her smock over her head and tossed it onto the table. "See," she said proudly. "Nice, huh?"

Louie opened his eyes and looked at her. "You're very beautiful, but I have to go."

"I want to thank you with my body," she said, leaning down so one of her breasts touched his cheek.

"Let me up," said Louie. "Please."

"You wanted this," she said, nodding. "If you didn't want it, you wouldn't have come."

"No," he said, wearily.

"Yes," she said, kissing him. She tried to force her tongue into his mouth, but he wouldn't let her. "Let me," she demanded. "You want it."

"I'm getting up," said Louie.

She laughed at him as he rolled over onto his stomach. With a great effort, he got up onto his knees. She hung on, riding him like a child on a grown-up's back.

"Get off," said Louie, "or you'll fall."

She refused to let go, forcing him to use all his strength to stand up. She stood behind him, her arms locked around his waist.

"Chris," he said, his voice shaky. "I can break your hold now. I don't want to hurt you, so please let me go."

"Why don't you want me?" she asked, sadly.

"I don't even know you."

"You got hard," she whined.

"I'm easy that way," he said. "Please let me go."

She released him, then punched him hard between his shoulder blades. Louie whirled around to block her blows, but she had moved to the bed. She picked up Ananda and put her in the crib beside her brother. Then she lay down on the bed and held out her arms to Louie.

110

"Come on, Louie," she said, spreading her legs. "Be a man."

"It has nothing to do with that," he said, turning to go.

"I have feelings, you know," she said, starting to cry.

Louie stopped at the door and turned to look at her. "You can *talk* about feelings."

"I'm not much of a talker," she said, holding her arms out again.

"I have to go," said Louie, opening the door.

"Come back if you want," she whispered.

"Goodbye," he said, going out.

111

Andrea

I was glad I'd come home, but now my house seemed absurdly large for one person. I wondered if Louie would like the way I lived, my taste in art, the color of my towels. I knew it wouldn't matter to him, but I wondered just the same.

So many things I had valued so highly were no longer important to me. I understood for the first time what Mother meant about measuring things by my father. Louie was more valuable than all my possessions.

But I retained the conscious thought that he might

never come. It was essential that I remind myself of
that. People die. People change. I'd opened up a part of
myself that had not been open for a long time, if ever,
but I wasn't foolish enough to believe that merely
because I wanted him, he would come.

I decided to clean my house. It was a task that
would benefit me, whether he came or not.

18.

Louie walked up the hill, leaving Gharkey Street and downtown Santa Cruz behind him. He went past the high school, where three girls in short skirts sat on top of the retaining wall that bordered the sidewalk. They were kicking their heels against the stones, pretending not to notice the long-haired boys playing Frisbee on the lawn behind them. A brisk breeze was blowing in from the sea, carrying with it the faint smell of seaweed. Louie smiled at the girls as he passed by, and one of them laughed and said, "Stoned."

"I'm not," Louie said to himself. "Just because I'm smiling, doesn't mean I'm stoned."

He walked slowly, stopping now and then to see where he was and to look at houses he was especially fond of, and then suddenly he found himself looking up at the house that used to be his, a three-story Victorian, backlit by the afternoon sun. "Still there," said Louie, stopping at the front gate and touching the picket fence.

A big Doberman, teeth bared, came slanting around the corner of the house, skidded to a halt at the fence, stuck his snout through the slats and growled ominously. "Jesus," said Louie, backing away. "I'm just looking, boy. Take it easy."

The rosebushes he'd planted beside the fence were enormous now, in need of pruning. The chimney he had so carefully restored had been removed. The new shingle roof was covered with a bank of solar panels. Louie stared at the roof, then at the front walk, and he realized that the bricks from the chimney had become the front path to the house. In the cracks between the bricks, sweet alyssum and chamomile were flourishing.

"Nice work," he said, turning away, overcome with sadness. But someone called his name, so softly it might have been his imagination endowing the wind with a voice. He turned and Marie was standing there by the front gate, holding the Doberman by the collar. She was dressed all in white, her long blond hair spilling over her shoulders like spun gold. Louie doubted what he saw, and was unable to speak.

"Welcome home," she said, gazing steadily at him. "I live here now. Come in." She opened the gate, then leaned down and told her dog to be good. When she released him, the dog walked stiffly to Louie and sniffed at him but didn't growl.

115

"I . . . I can't believe you're here," Louie said, not moving.

"Please come in," she said, turning toward the house.

Louie took a few tentative steps, then stopped. "I . . . Marie? How did you . . ."

She continued up the front walk, the dog trotting after her. Louie moved slowly into the yard, closing the gate behind him, realizing as he did so that he had done it the same way a thousand times before.

"You sure are skinny," she said, turning to him at the front door. "Don't you eat anymore?"

"Sometimes," he said, looking up at the house. "I'm standing on the chimney, aren't I?"

"Yes," she said, lowering her eyes. "It's real different inside, too. I knocked out some walls, added lots of windows. I hope you like it."

"It always needed that," he said, shoving his hands into his pockets. "Marie?"

"You're sure skinnier," she said, opening the door quickly and going in.

The living room, dining room, and kitchen had become one enormous room, with thick oriental carpets covering most of the hardwood floors. There was an ebony grand piano in one corner of the room, surrounded by tall potted ferns. There were elegant chairs and a couch, with frames made of rounded redwood and cushions of white silk.

"My god," said Louie, sitting on the piano bench, his back to the keyboard. "Did you do all this?"

"You like it?" she asked, setting the teakettle on the huge black deco stove that stood amidst dark teak cabinets and dangling copper pots at the kitchen end of the room. The floor there was done in large brown Spanish tiles.

"It's amazing," he said, shaking his head and frowning.

"Upstairs is pretty much the same as when you lived here," she said, folding her arms and watching the kettle, "except I put in a couple more skylights. And I tiled the bathrooms. You always said they should be tiled."

"It's wonderful," he said, standing up. "I can't believe it."

"I can't believe you haven't touched me," she said, trembling.

Louie crossed the room to her, hesitated, then put his arms around her. Feeling how light she was, he lifted her off the ground.

"Put me down," she said, holding her body rigid. "Put me down."

Marie

He put me down and I slapped him across the face. He stepped back and looked at me in that way men look when they're deciding whether to fight or run, and then he moved to me and slipped his arms around my waist, but I couldn't stand it, so I hit him again. He held on, and all I could think of was to keep hitting him until he let go. And then I started to say things, filthy things, and I kept hitting him. His nose started bleeding, so he released me. But that wasn't enough, so I went after him and punched him in the stomach, but my arms were tired, so I kicked him, and I kept kicking him until he hit me.

118

I wasn't expecting it. I don't think he was either, but it was good he did, because I was so far gone I didn't know what I was doing. I was hurting him worse than I knew, kicking his wound, and he swung out blindly to stop me, instead of running. His fist caught me in the throat and I went down hard on my butt. He stood there, hunched over, his body shaking, looking down on me with such pain in his face, I couldn't believe he wouldn't cry. I saw the blood pouring from his leg and I didn't know what to do, because I wanted to help him, but I wanted him to be hurt, too.

He limped into the kitchen, so the blood fell on the tile instead of on my rug, and his doing that changed everything for me. It seemed like such an unselfish thing for him to do.

He must have seen me change, because he sat down and tended to his wound. I got up and came into the kitchen to make ice packs for both of us. He let me help him out to the back deck, though he tried not to lean on me too much. We got his leg propped up, and I peeled back his pants leg to check the damage. It was a mess, so I went in and called my doctor. He said to bring Louie down, that he'd squeeze him in.

It was so strange, because we both wanted to talk, but neither of us could. I drove him to the clinic, sat with him while they cleaned him up and repaired the stitches, and then I drove him home and helped him out to the deck again. Neither of us said a word to each other the whole time.

Finally I asked him to stay for supper. He nodded that he would. I left a note for my kids, explaining who Louie was, and then I left. I just drove around, staying off the busy streets, trying to calm down. When that didn't work, I went over to the yacht harbor and sat on my boat. Then I went grocery shopping because that usually makes me feel better.

19.

Marie's eight-year-old son Cal came out onto the deck, holding the note his mother had left for him. He had straight blond hair, big brown eyes, round cheeks and radiantly white teeth. He was wearing blue tennis shoes, blue jeans, a blue T-shirt and a blue jacket.

"Hi," said Louie. "I'm Louie."

"I know," said Cal, sneering slightly. "It's in the note."

"You must be Cal, or do they call you Blue?"

"Very funny," said Cal, looking at the note. "Do you need anything to drink?"

120

"No," said Louie, "I'm fine."

Cal came closer and looked at Louie's leg, started to ask about it, then changed his mind. "Well, I have soccer practice," he said imperiously, "and I think she forgot, because, see, my sister can't read very well, she's only six, and I have to go before she gets home, because the coach makes you run laps if you're late."

"I'll explain to your sister who I am," said Louie, shifting his leg, "or do you think she'll be frightened?"

"No," said Cal, "she's not afraid of anything, but she can read easy words, so maybe I'll write her an easy note."

That proved unnecessary, as Eva arrived a moment later, snatched the note from her brother and read it aloud easily. She was a pert, pretty little girl, immensely self-assured and far more sophisticated than Louie thought six-year-old girls were supposed to be. Her golden hair was tied in a ponytail and she was wearing a rainbow colored T-shirt, khaki pants and very fancy purple running shoes, all of which gave her the appearance of a miniature fashion model.

Cal went inside to put on his soccer clothes, while Eva brought Louie a snack of cookies and lemonade, which she shared with him. They discussed school, which she loved, because Mrs. Bellinger was *so* wonderful, and her girlfriend, Carol, whom she loved because she was *so* funny, and her brother, whom she adored because he was *so* good at everything.

"You know," said Eva, taking the last cookie, "maybe you should marry my mother." Then she jumped up from her chair and did a handstand. "I take gymnastics," she said, upside down, her face turning red. "She's very beautiful, isn't she?"

"Yes," said Louie, nodding. "And so are you."

"So," said Eva, doing a walkover, then quickly

straightening her T-shirt, "wouldn't you like to marry her?"

"We hardly know each other," said Louie. "You want to know someone really well before you marry them."

"She talks about you all the time," said Eva, putting her hand on her hip.

"We haven't seen each other in a long time," said Louie.

"Do I remember you?" she asked, leaning on the arm of his chair and squinting at him.

"The last time I saw you, you were two," he said. "You called me Wooie."

"Does Cal remember you?"

"I don't think so. He doesn't seem to."

"Excuse me," she said, running into the house.

The Doberman came up onto the deck and sniffed at Louie, but when Louie reached to pet him, the dog shied away, growling. Eva returned, running on her toes, a photo album under her arm.

"You run like a ballerina," said Louie, smiling at her.

"I take ballet, gymnastics, ice skating, and piano," she said haughtily.

"When do you sleep?" he asked, feigning astonishment.

"At night, of course," she said, opening the photo album and giving him one end of it.

There was Louie, in a blurry color photo, sitting at the old black upright piano at the Seaside Inn. Bill Isaacs stood to one side, towering over his big bass, while tiny Andy Willis sat amidst his drums, his eyes closed, an ecstatic smile on his face.

"That's us," said Louie. "I wonder what we were playing."

Eva turned the page, and there was Marie, sitting on the piano bench beside Louie, her arm around him. She was turned profile, singing, her mouth just inches from Louie's ear.

Then came a picture of the four of them, all in a row, Bill, Marie, Louie and Andy, their arms around each other.

"I remember the night we took those pictures," said Louie, looking at Eva, "but I don't remember who took them."

"And, um, one more," said Eva, turning the page.

Louie and Marie were holding each other on the dance floor at the Coconut Grove. Her face was tilted up toward his and they seemed to be on the verge of a kiss.

"Those are nice," said Louie, looking away from the picture.

"She has a poster of that one in her bedroom," said Eva, shutting the album. "Wanta see it?"

"I'm supposed to keep my leg up," he said, raising his hands in despair.

"We could play cards," she said, arching an eyebrow. "Do you know Fish?"

"Is that anything like Do-You-Have-This?"

"Yes," she said, frowning, "except you don't have to say, do you have, uh, say, fives. You just say '*Any* fives,' and if he doesn't have any, he says 'Fish.' "

"Sure," said Louie gravely. "I think I can handle that."

Eva gave him a cautionary look. "But if he *does* have a five, then he gives it to you and you get another turn, and also . . ." She paused for a moment, concentrating. "If you ask for fives and he says 'Fish' and I take a card and it *is* a five, then I say 'Got one,' and then I get another turn."

123

"Get the cards," said Louie rubbing his hands together.

"We also have some pictures of me when I was a baby," she said, going in. 'You want to see those instead?"

"Cards," said Louie. "I'm feeling lucky."

Eva

We played Fish. I think he cheated sometimes so I could win, because one time I forgot he had jacks and I got a jack and I think he saw it. Then he said, if only I had one more jack, so I asked him for jacks and he slapped his forehead and said, Oh no! because then I got a book. And then he taught me Concentration, where you lay out all the cards, but it got too windy and they started blowing all over the place.

20.

An older Mexican woman, Flora, arrived in the late afternoon to do some ironing and prepare dinner. She came out on the deck, said hello to Louie and told Eva it was time to practice the piano. Louie came inside and listened to Eva work through some easy Kabalevsky, which she played slowly, but with surprising feeling. Cal came home, boasting of his heroism on the soccer field. Flora told him to take a bath. He obeyed instantly, as did Eva when told to wash up for dinner.

"You have these children well trained," said Louie,

resting comfortably on the couch, his leg elevated on a pile of Persian pillows.

"I don't do nothing," said Flora, carrying dishes and silverware to the table. "Es su madre. She very strict." She looked at Louie for a moment, trying to think how to express her feelings in English. "She's a good mother. Everything is for them." She wiped her hands on her apron. "Es posible you play el piano. Un concierto? The children hear all the time about you . . . tocando?"

Louie limped to the piano, sat down on the bench, rested his hands on the keys for a moment, and then began to play. He started with a simple waltz, spiking it with jazzy trills, then he jumped into a sassy blues that rushed along and became a fancy samba that trailed off into a series of deep, lush minor chords that completed the medley.

Eva and Cal, sitting on the couch together, applauded loudly. Marie was standing in the dining area, sipping a glass of red wine. Flora was carrying a steaming casserole to the table, smiling to herself.

"Time flies," said Louie, cracking his knuckles as he turned away from the keyboard. "I didn't hear you come in."

"Ooh gross," said Eva, shuddering. "Doesn't that hurt?"

"No," said Cal matter-of-factly. "All piano players do that." He looked to Louie for confirmation.

"Mr. Lenowitz doesn't," said Eva, standing up. "And *he* plays with the symphony."

"Maybe not in front of *you*," said Cal, reddening.

"Not in front of *you* either," said Eva, jutting out her chin defiantly.

"How do *you* know?" said Cal, clenching his fists.

"Hey," said Louie, intervening, "you guys know

127

this one?" He banged out eight bars of the *Star Wars* theme.

"Dinner," whispered Marie, swirling her wine.

"Mom lost her voice," said Eva, going to the table.

Louie stood up and limped across the room. When he got to the table he mouthed the words 'I'm sorry' to Marie. She mouthed them back to him.

"No secrets at the dinner table," said Eva, looking first at Louie, then at her mother.

Cal held Eva's chair for her, then did the same for Flora. Louie held Marie's chair for her, waited for Cal to sit, then took his place at the head of the table.

"Will you say the blessing, please?" asked Cal, looking at Louie, before bowing his head. Eva closed her eyes and sighed. Flora crossed herself and put a hand to her forehead. Louie glanced at Marie, she smiled slightly, closed her eyes and clasped her hands together.

Louie looked down at his plate and cleared his throat. "Please, God," he said quietly, "bless this wonderful food. And bless these wonderful people and this beautiful house. Thank you."

"Amen," whispered Marie.

"Amen," said Cal, giving Louie a strange look.

"That was different," said Eva, unfolding her napkin. "Um, are you Catholic?"

"No," said Louie, sipping his wine.

"What are you?" asked Cal.

"I don't know," said Louie. "What are you?"

"Catholic," said Cal, shrugging. "Obviously."

"So am I," said Eva, nodding.

"He *knows* that," said Cal, glaring at her.

"Eat," whispered Marie.

"Usually we have gymnastics and karate," said Eva, a noodle dangling from her mouth, "but tonight is a special night because you're here."

128

"I'm honored," said Louie, glancing at Marie.

"Tienen vestidos very pretty," said Flora, smiling at Eva.

"*I* take karate," said Cal, gulping his milk. "Wait'll you see my gi."

"Eso," said Flora, pointing at Cal. "El gi."

"Wait'll you see *my* leotard," said Eva, giving Cal a superior look. "It's burgundy."

"Big deal," said Cal, fidgeting in his seat. "Who cares?"

"Louie cares," said Eva, nodding to herself. "That's who."

Marie

I kept wondering why he came back, though I always knew he would. I wondered why he was being so good to my children if he didn't intend to stay. He talked to them like he planned to know them in the future, and it made me want to grab him and say, "Listen Louie, don't get our hopes up again." But there was another part of me that thought, "Go on, Louie, get yourself in deep, tangle yourself up with my kids and my life so deeply you'll never be able to leave."

21.

When Flora was gone and the children were in bed, Marie and Louie sat in the living room, drinking wine and trying to talk.

"You want to put your leg up?" she asked, looking sadly at him.

"No," he said, "it feels okay."

"You want to see some pictures?"

"Eva showed me some already," he said, speaking quietly to match her whispering.

"Not those," said Marie, blushing slightly. "She

keeps those in her room. I meant pictures of things since you've been gone."

"I'd love to," he said, "though I'm still having a hard time believing I'm here with you. I'm dying to know how you got this place."

"The pictures don't show that," she said, getting up. "I'm gonna have to tell you about that."

She went upstairs to get the photographs, while Louie hobbled into the kitchen to pour himself some more wine. He stood at the stove, looking out over the room, admiring the spaciousness she'd achieved, when it dawned on him that many of the modifications Marie had made were ones that he had envisioned for the house years before. This realization so amazed him that he forgot to pour himself more wine, and returned to his chair with an empty glass.

Marie came down the stairs slowly, savoring the fact of Louie's presence. She handed him the photo album, started to sit down beside him, but then changed her mind. "I'm gonna take a shower," she said, turning away. "I'll be down in a bit."

The first photos in the album were of the babies in front of a little house in Capitola, where they lived with their Uncle Bill while Marie was in prison. Then there were a few shots of Marie in Soledad: hamming it up with her girlfriends in the cafeteria, playing volleyball, melodramatically clutching the bars of a cell, holding her kids in the visiting room. There was one picture taken on the day of her release. She was wearing a rumpled dress, her hair was cut short and she looked tired and disappointed.

Then there were pictures of the kids and Marie on the beach, the kids at school, the kids on the merry-go-round, Marie working at the cannery, Marie waiting tables at the Seaside Inn, the kids dressed as clowns on

132

Halloween. Then a year or so went unchronicled, and suddenly Marie was uprooting the *For Sale* sign in front of Louie's house, the renovation began, the kids posed in front of their new Volvo station wagon, Eva took ballet, Cal put on his gi, Marie went to rug auctions in San Francisco, bought a Doberman pup, took the kids sailing and planted sunflowers and tomatoes in the back yard.

"It's a mystery," said Louie, looking up at Marie as she came down the stairs.

She'd changed into blue silk pajamas. Her hair was tied back in a ponytail and her face was scrubbed clean of makeup. She had always been beautiful, but in the three years that Louie had been gone, her beauty had deepened, her movements had become more graceful. The poor girl from Texas had been transformed into a woman of refinement.

"I have to tell you, Louie," she said, whispering to him from the foot of the stairs. "But I'm going to ask you to do something first. It may seem kind of silly, but I need you to."

"What?" he said, closing the album.

"Well," she said, taking a few steps toward him, "I bought a pair of pajamas like this for you, for when we were together again. I'd like you to put them on, and then I'll tell you everything. Will you do that?"

Marie

In some ways, anyway, my dream was coming true. Louie was in my house, his house, lying on my bed, staring up at the stained-glass skylights. All I had to do was tell him how I got the money, and see if he could still love me after he knew.

None of it seems real to me anymore, except Edgar sometimes, and being so sick in Buenos Aires. I only remember the first old guy I jerked off at the Dream Inn because he was the first, not because he was memorable. I don't even know what made me go with him, except I was tired of being a cocktail waitress, getting my ass pinched for three bucks an hour and lousy tips, and I needed more money. Suddenly it was easy to go, to say yes, to unzip them, to do them one way or the other, it didn't matter which, because it never took very long and I was always so loaded I couldn't feel anything anyway.

So when they fired me for tricking, I just moved up a notch, or down, depending on where you're looking from, and I started working the lounges, still mostly doing the quick, cheap stuff, but occasionally balling a guy if he insisted and had the money. I stuck with the older guys, because they were predictable and easy. They just wanted someone to make love to their cocks because their wives wouldn't.

But then I got beat up, the second time I hooked somebody younger, and I was so scared I stayed home for a week. Then I went out and tried to get a regular job again, but nothing had changed and nobody wanted a convicted felon, especially since some people still remembered the trial.

So I took a job in a massage parlor, to have some protection, but after I got done paying for the room and giving a cut to the manager and the bouncer, and paying for my cocaine, I didn't have much left over, no matter how many men I processed.

I went back to the lounges and stuck to the older guys, and I did okay, I made a living, but I was getting old fast. I'd come home about two or three in the morning, take a downer so I could sleep, and just black out for ten hours. I'd drag myself out of bed in time to pick the kids up at school, bring them home, make them supper, then get ready to go out again. The babysitter came at eight, and off I'd go.

My brother Billy didn't come around much once I started tricking. He was sick about it, and every week or so he'd call me up and beg me to move with him somewhere new, where I could start over. He didn't understand my sickness, or even that I *was* sick.

Then one night I was sitting in the Crow's Nest at the yacht harbor, watching the big boats gliding in and out, wishing I was on one, when the waitress came up to me and said there was someone who wanted to see me. I tipped her five, went to the bathroom, got my face right, popped a little speed and came out to check my trick. I was expecting a lonely businessman with white hair, a big belly and quick hands. They're all the same guy, with the same wife they haven't loved since she stopped being a pretty girl.

But Edgar was from a different universe than those men. He'd never had a wife, except maybe his boat, and love was something he reserved for food and wine and diamonds. Life was a game to him, like chess, and people were pawns mostly, though some were rooks or bishops, and a few were queens. Edgar was the king, except he could move any way he wanted and take any other piece.

He was a huge man, tall and obese, and bald. He always wore a kimono, and he was wearing one that night in the Crow's Nest. Everybody in the place was staring at him. I wouldn't have dared approach him, but he sent Lek, his strange little valet, to invite me to have dinner with them. When I hesitated, Lek gave me a hundred-dollar bill and assured me they just wanted to talk. I figured I'd be safe as long as we stayed in the restaurant, so I went.

Edgar was from Argentina, but he spoke English with a very slight British accent. He told me he'd been watching me for a couple of weeks. He knew where I lived, where my kids went to school, that I'd been in prison. He even knew about Louie. He called me the perfect fallen angel, just what he'd been looking for. When I asked him what he meant, he started talking about Greek myths and Inca myths, and how I embodied the ultimate irony of existence. He said I was physically perfect, yet wholly corruptible. I appeared to be pure, even virginal he said, but I was a whore, only he used the Greek word *hetaera,* and said he would make me into a modern day Phryne, which meant he was going to pay me a lot of money to do whatever he wanted me to do.

I couldn't look at Louie while I told him all this. I stood at the window, looking out at the trees and the rooftops, trying to make it a story about somebody I knew, and not me, which in a way it was, because it seemed like it had happened to somebody else. I hadn't touched anybody in almost two years. My body had forgotten just about everything, even if I could still remember how horrible it all was.

Louie didn't say anything. I don't think he moved once the whole time I talked, and I talked for a long time.

I told him about going to my lawyer with Edgar, working out a contract for the trip, sitting there with the same man who'd defended me, selling myself to Edgar for six months of slavery. I was to be called his assistant and available to him twenty-four hours a day, for which I would receive more money than I ever dreamed of.

I remember going into the bank the next day, high on cocaine, with an advance check for twenty-five thousand dollars, actually feeling like I deserved it, that it was my due. And then I got in touch with Billy and talked him into taking the kids again. Two days later I went on board Edgar's boat, the *Bucephalus,* named after Alexander the Great's horse.

When we got to Los Angeles a few days later, I was in ecstasy. So far, all we'd done was talk about art and mythology, eat fine food, watch the water and sleep. I was left to sleep alone at night. Edgar told me there would be parties—festivals, he called them—and I'd have to do whatever was asked of me then. But I had no way of anticipating what was going to happen, because everything I knew was based on working the lounges. I couldn't imagine it being much more than an exaggeration of the same kind of need I ran into there.

But it was more than that. I don't really know how to describe it, because it *was* sex, but it was with such strange people, in such horrible ways, without there ever being even the pretense of love or tenderness. It was as if Edgar and all his friends lived their whole lives to destroy love, to make it into something hideous.

One time, in Acapulco, in a big stone house overlooking the harbor, they had me chained to the floor, and I'd been there for so long all the drugs and booze had worn off, and they wouldn't even let me up to go to the bathroom. I was shivering and crying and begging them to let me go, but Edgar wasn't there to help me. These three big men sat around me in armchairs, smoking hash, taking turns doing things to me. One would beat me with ropes, one spat on me, peed on me, and one of them curled up beside me and suckled on me until my breasts were raw. After that, after I locked myself in my cabin for two days, Edgar agreed I could always have my drugs, that no matter what anyone wanted to do to me, they had to let me go to the bathroom and they had to let me take whatever I needed to get through it.

Edgar loved to talk to me. He knew so much about so many things, and he got a big thrill out of educating his little *chère amie,* which was one of his favorite euphemisms for whore. We would sit on the deck, sipping our drinks, and he'd talk about history and perversity and his childhood in Argentina. Sometimes he'd take me in his lap and cuddle me and promise me he'd never let anyone hurt me, until we came to the next stop and he'd trade me again. He called me his golden chit. Now and then he'd stay to watch what happened to me, and that's when he'd cry, seeing them defile me, but he never intervened.

In Santiago, I was given something to drink, I don't know what, something that made me lose control of my arms and legs, so I was like an epileptic, and when I screamed for help, the man just laughed and let me flop around on the floor.

Then we'd be back on the boat, resting, talking, like a weird couple on a pleasure cruise. But I started to lose it. I couldn't sleep anymore and I had to take more and more drugs just to keep going. I wasn't going to make it to Buenos Aires if I got any worse, and Edgar knew it.

So he cancelled the next few stops and we sailed day and night to Buenos Aires, to Edgar's big house on the coast. He put me to bed and nursed me, trying to make me strong. I think, in his own incredibly twisted way, he loved me. I was always in too much pain to love him, though he was a brilliant man and seemed to understand things about me that nobody else ever had.

When I was better, though not really well, he took me to the last party, my last and final labor, he called it. Somewhere on the outskirts of the city—I don't know where because I was so coked up I was almost happy— we came to a big villa. Everyone there was wearing these amazing colored costumes and plumed head-dresses, like Inca gods. Edgar gave me over to a group of women. They took me to a secluded spot by a fountain, where they stripped me. Then they cut their fingers and rubbed me with their blood. Then they carried me through a forest to a clearing where all the other people were gathered around a sacrificial stone, and I knew they were going to cut my heart out and I'd never see my children again, or Louie, or anything. Not that it should have mattered anymore. Nothing should have mattered, but it did. I wanted to live.

So I fought, but I wasn't strong enough. They dragged me to the altar and held me down. Then Edgar came out with a beautiful young man and they stood looking down at me, chanting something I couldn't understand. Edgar's whole body was shaking, his eyes were quivering, like he was in a trance, and then the young man leaned down and licked me for a long time until I was wet enough to receive him, but then Edgar entered me, fell on me, and with all the people shouting, he fucked me.

When I turned to look at Louie, he was frozen, staring into space. Then he came out of his daze a little and moved over to make room for me on the bed. I turned off the light, lay down beside him, and he put his arms around me and held me. He didn't say anything, but I could feel that it was taking all his strength even to touch me.

22.

Louie came down the stairs, looking sleepy and sad. The children had left for school. Marie was in the kitchen, making waffles for breakfast. She was wearing white shorts and a man's dress shirt tailored to her woman's body. "Did you finally sleep?" she asked, looking up from the stove.

"This morning," he said, sitting down at the piano. "You?"

"I slept like a log," she said, nodding. "My voice came back, too."

Louie played a few quiet chords, then got up and

walked into the kitchen. "Marie?" he said, shoving his hands into his pocket.

"What?" she said, turning to him.

"I don't know what to do."

"About what?"

"About you," he said, taking a step toward her.

"I want you to stay," she said, gazing steadily at him. "I want you."

"But Marie," he said, shaking his head, "how can you after what's happened?"

"It's not a matter of me," she said, going to him. "It's whether *you* want to." She put her arms around him and rested her head on his shoulder.

"There's a woman I met recently," Louie began, but Marie put a finger to his lips to keep him from going on.

"Don't," she said, shaking her head, "unless you're going to stay for a while." She looked up at him. "I think you owe me that, don't you?"

"Yes," he said, closing his eyes.

"Isn't that why you came back?"

"I came back to see you and Joanna."

"Joanna?" said Marie. "You're in for a surprise, Louie."

"Why?" he asked, opening his eyes.

"She's very different now," said Marie, going back to the waffle iron. "Let's eat outside, okay?"

"I guess I could stay for a day or so," Louie murmured.

"Only if you want to," said Marie, smiling to herself

142

Marie

I was going to take him to bed, if I could, right after breakfast. I'd planned on making love with him the night before, but he was too upset, and I probably was, too. But when he said he wanted to see Joanna, I decided to wait, so that when he came back he'd be able to love me without wondering about her.

Still, it was hard to let him go, to believe him when he said he'd be back. When he left, I went out in the garden and turned the soil for a long time, trying to calm down, but eventually I resorted to wine and got drunk long before noon.

23.

Joanna lived south of downtown near the beach, but Louie drove west, up Empire Grade, until he was high above the city. Then he turned the Mercedes around and rolled down the hill, the brilliant blue bay below him, the Monterey peninsula rising above the haze in the distance. It was as if he needed a running start to make it through town again. He drove across the San Lorenzo River, past the boardwalk with its rumbling roller coaster, over the yacht harbor bridge and around Twin Lakes Beach to Fourteenth Avenue, where he stopped beside a small white cottage.

"My God," he said to himself, "she still has the Volkswagen." It had been their first and only car, a 1965 convertible bug. Originally green, it had been repainted a dark brown, the white convertible top replaced by a khaki one, giving the car the look of a miniature combat vehicle.

Louie sat looking at the Volkswagen for a few minutes, then he got out of the Mercedes, made sure his shirt was tucked in, smoothed back his hair and walked to the front door.

Before he could knock, the door swung open. A big-hipped, big-bosomed woman with long brown hair stood before him. She had deep-set brown eyes, a slightly crooked nose, heavy lips and wide cheeks. "Yes?" she said, her voice deep and husky.

"I'm looking for Joanna," he said, swallowing nervously.

"Joanna's working," said the woman, giving Louie a curious look. "What did you want to see her about?"

Louie cleared his throat. "I'm her ex-husband," he began, "and I was in town, so I thought . . ."

"I thought you looked familiar," she said, nodding. "I've seen pictures." She folded her arms and sighed heavily. "You really should have called first."

"I can come back."

"No," she said. "Just wait a minute and I'll tell her you're here."

Louie put his hands in his pockets and turned his back to the door. The front yard of the little house was lush with nasturtiums and blackberries. Louie reached out to pick a big berry, but stopped himself when he heard the woman returning.

He followed her through the tiny house and out into the back yard. There was a small vegetable garden near the side fence, but the rest of the yard was filled with large pieces of stone, metal and wood. Wood chips, iron scraps, and fragments of rock covered the ground. Here and there, a scraggly lawn survived.

In the center of the yard, a woman wearing overalls and goggles was directing the fire of an acetylene torch at a joint in a towering structure of interwoven steel rods. As Louie approached her, she turned off her torch and raised the goggles from her eyes.

Joanna's hair, once long and brown, was now cropped close to her head and streaked with grey. Her petiteness had given way to a muscular robustness, and her languid movements had been supplanted by firm, definite gestures. Her soft round cheeks had melted away, and her features had sharpened, giving her beauty a fierceness that no smile could completely mitigate.

Joanna held out her hand to Louie, making it clear she wanted to shake, not hug. "So like you not to call first," she said tersely.

"I'm sorry," he said.

"It's all right," she said, meeting his gaze. "This is better. I probably would have said not to come."

"I'm going in," said the other woman, calling from the back door. "If you need anything, let me know."

"Did you introduce yourself?" asked Joanna.

"No," said the woman, bowing her head slightly.

"This is Erma," said Joanna.

"Hello," said Louie, nodding to her.

"Hello," she said, blushing. "I'll be inside."

"Well, what do you think of it?" asked Joanna, turning to her sculpture.

"It's very graceful," said Louie, gesturing. "I like the way it bends." He laughed. "It reminds me just a little of that thing we built on the mudflats in Berkeley."

"I'd forgotten about that," said Joanna, nodding. "I

146

was trying to remember all the things that might have led me to this." She smiled sardonically. "Of course, I'd blocked out most of the things connected with you."

"You were always an artist," said Louie.

"Now he tells me," she said softly.

"I told you," he said, frowning at her. "I always told you."

"You spoke words," said Joanna, shaking her head. "Your tone implied otherwise."

They stood silently for a moment, Louie looking at her sculpture, Joanna looking at Louie.

"What do you want, Louie?" she asked, leaning back against the lattice of steel rods.

"I don't know," he said, shrugging. "I needed to see you."

"And then what?"

"I don't know. Talk, I guess."

Joanna shook her head. "About what? About the past, about how everything is better now, everything forgiven? Forget it, Louie. You'll just have to learn to live with the bad memories, too. They don't go away. They recede a little, that's all."

"I hoped they would go away," he said, taking a step toward her.

She tensed. "You would, Louie."

"I understand you now," he said, frowning. "Or at least I understand why things happened, and I wanted to tell you, I don't blame you anymore."

"Good," she said coldly. "That's very adult of you. I don't blame you either. Now that we've absolved each other, I think you should leave."

"I really do like this sculpture," he said, smiling at her. "It's growing like a plant."

"I'm glad you like it," she said, lowering the

goggles over her eyes. "You always had excellent taste."

"Well, goodbye," he said, turning to go. Then he turned back to her.

She stood poised, ready to relight her torch. "What?" she asked.

"You really don't want to talk any more?" he asked, sadly.

"I really didn't want to see you at all," she replied.

Eva

I ran all over looking for Louie, but he was gone. Mom said he was coming back tonight, but then he called and said tomorrow. I wanted to talk to him, and at first Mom said no, but then she said okay, so I told him my friend Carol wanted to meet him. Then he asked me how my friend Jim was, and I said Jim who, and he said Jim Nastics. So Cal and I tried to do that with other things, but Jim Nastics was the best.

149

24.

Louie stopped at the market to buy food and flowers for Helen. He called her from the store to find out what she needed, but no one answered the phone at Pajaro, so he only bought a half-dozen carnations and the fixings for a shrimp salad.

When he got to the house, Buka was outside, scratching at the front door. Louie let the dog in, put the groceries and flowers in the kitchen, then hurried down the hall to Helen's room where Buka was scratching frantically at the door.

"Helen?" he said, loudly. "Are you there?"

No one answered. Louie tried to force the door, but it wouldn't budge. He ran down the hall, out the back door and around to the side of the house. He tried to open her windows, but they were locked. He dashed back into the house, found a screwdriver and a hammer, then ran back outside. He tried to force one of the windows, but the hinges were on the inside and it wouldn't give. He broke the glass, unlocked the window, pulled it open and crawled into the room.

Helen was sprawled on the floor. She was naked save for a scarf tied loosely around her neck. Her eyes were closed, her face was colorless and she was barely breathing. Louie grabbed the bedside phone and called an ambulance, then he sat Helen up and slapped her cheeks a few times. There was no response. He put his arm around her shoulders and stuck a finger in her mouth, forcing it down her throat, but she wasn't breathing enough for this to have any effect. He put his head on her chest for a moment, then searched her face for signs of life. A siren sounded in the distance and Buka began to howl with it. Louie lay Helen down on the floor, tilted her head back, pried open her mouth and breathed into her.

Helen

The stale air came into my lungs, waking me, pulling me back from the edge, ruining my escape. Still, I hoped I was waking into another world, that it would be George above me, pulling me from one dimension into another. When I saw Louie, I shut my eyes and tried to will myself dead. But then the blue boys arrived and overwhelmed my dying with their damned oxygen.

152

25.

Louie followed the ambulance to the hospital in Watsonville and stayed close to Helen in the emergency room until the doctor told him she was out of danger. Then he drove back to Pajaro, fed Buka, made himself a pot of coffee and sat down to call Andrea.

He stared at the phone for a minute or two, then got up and went out onto the deck to watch the sun setting. A chilly wind was knifing in from the sea, making it feel like winter again. Buka left his food and came to Louie, hoping for some attention.

"I could leave," said Louie, reaching down to scratch the dog's head. "You could come with me. You'd love it. We could follow the apple harvest all the way from here to Canada, and then we could hitch down to Mexico for the winter. Lots of dogs in Mexico. They might not let you in. We might have to go to Arizona."

Satisfied with the head massage, Buka went back to his food. Louie leaned on the railing and watched the wind-whipped waves rolling into shore. "Yeah," he said, nodding, "we could just get the hell out of here and go someplace quiet and warm."

He went inside and started a fire, poured himself a fresh cup of coffee and settled himself in the rocking chair. He misdialed Andrea's number the first time, waking up an old lady with a thick southern accent. He dialed more carefully the second time and Andrea answered on the second ring.

"I just wrote you," she said, breathlessly, sounding very close.

"Did I interrupt something?" he asked, nervously.

"No, I just this minute finished the letter, and the phone rang and I'm just surprised." She paused, waiting for him to speak. When he didn't, she asked, "How are you?"

"Well," said Louie, gripping the phone tightly, "I'm okay, but Helen isn't doing so well."

"What do you mean?" said Andrea, raising her voice. "I just spoke to her this morning."

"Well, she . . . she took an overdose of sleeping pills, but they say she's going to be okay. She's in the hospital now. I just came from there."

"I'll fly out tomorrow morning," said Andrea, her voice fading slightly. "I should never have left."

"There was no way to know," he said. "She was in great spirits when I left here, too."

"She's a great actress," said Andrea, sighing. "I'm sorry, Louie. This is just what you needed, right?"

"Apparently I got to her pretty soon after she lost consciousness, so the doctors are pretty sure there won't be any brain damage."

"Good," said Andrea. "I can probably be out there by tomorrow afternoon. Have you seen the people in Santa Cruz?"

"The people," said Louie, shrugging. "I'm in the midst of it. It's a little more complicated than I thought it would be."

"It always is," she said, sounding closer again. "But I still want you to come out here. You still want to come, don't you?"

"I'm terrible on the phone," said Louie, grimacing. "Shall I pick you up at the airport?"

"No," Andrea said. "I'll rent a car. You've done enough."

"Andrea . . ."

"We'll talk when I get there."

Louie stared at the phone, dead in its cradle, then picked it up and called Marie. She, too, was breathless when she answered.

"Well," she said, laughing, "I may never *see* you again, but you sure do call a lot."

"I . . . I think I'll come over there tonight," he said quickly, "if that's okay."

"You sound upset," she said gently. "Should I make you supper?"

"No," he said, "I'll grab something on the way."

"It's no trouble, honey."

"I don't know exactly when I'll be there," he said tersely.

"Just come over," she said calmly. "We'll work it out when you get here.

155

Marie

I could hear it in his voice. It was time for a master move, as Edgar called it. If I wanted Louie, I would have to do everything and say everything in just the right way, so he couldn't possibly turn me down.

26.

Damn you," said Helen, her voice gruff from the medication they'd given her.

Louie stood at the foot of her hospital bed, holding the carnations he'd intended to give her earlier that day.

"I *knew* you were psychic," said Helen, struggling to sit up. "Did you hear me, or just feel it?"

Louie dropped the flowers on the bed and went to help her. He put a couple pillows behind her, and she lay back heavily against them. She shut her eyes and he put a hand on her forehead. It was hot to the touch, so he rang for a nurse.

"They'll only give me another drug," said Helen, wrinkling her nose. "What the hell for, Louie? I'm old and I want to die. What's so horrible about that?"

"You're depressed," he said, sitting beside her. "When you get over being sad, you'll be happy you're alive."

"Nonsense," said Helen, smirking at him. "I'm very close to dotage. I hate that word, and I hate the thought of it." She clutched at Louie and looked around the room, her eyes wide with fright. "*I* want to die. I don't want some vestige of myself doing it. That was George's great accomplishment. *He* died. Do you see what I mean, Louie? Dying isn't bad if you're you when you do it. It's the loss of self *before* death that makes it so hideous."

"You sound fairly lucid to me," said Louie, winking at her.

"Death brings things into focus," she said, taking his hand. "Did you hear me or did you feel it?"

"It was a coincidence," he said, frowning at her. "I just happened to come back then."

"Don't be afraid of your powers," she said, her eyes burning into his. "I had *just* taken the pills. I had called to you out loud and in my mind, because I was afraid and I wanted you to hold me until I was gone."

"I didn't hear you, Helen," he said, bowing his head.

"Then why did you come back?" she asked, lifting his face so he had to look at her.

"To see you," he said, "to talk to you, to ask you to help me."

Helen caressed Louie's cheek and smiled sweetly at him. "You see how perfect it is. I needed you and you needed me."

"You missed a great shrimp salad," said Louie, scowling at her.

"That will be my second greatest regret," she said, letting go of him. "My first being that you didn't come an hour later."

A nurse bustled in and Louie moved out of the way so she could feel Helen's forehead, check her i.v. line and take her temperature with a digital thermometer. She seemed concerned about the digits and hurried out of the room.

"Maybe I'll have a stroke," said Helen, smiling happily. "*Then* you'll be sorry."

"Don't say that," said Louie, sitting beside her again.

"Denial is a very complicated business," she said, patting Louie's leg. "A peculiarly human trait." She wrinkled her nose again and sneezed. "George used to say that all the time. Animals are greedy and jealous and get very angry and very sad, but they are very bad at denying things. Indeed, they may not even know what that is." She sneezed again, reached for a Kleenex and said, "I think I'm allergic to hospitals. Can you take me home now?"

"Tomorrow," said Louie, "when Andrea comes. They want to observe you overnight."

"Ha!" said Helen, waving the idea away. "They want to put me to sleep until my daughter comes to remove the carcass."

"I'll see you tomorrow," said Louie, kissing her.

"All right, dear," she said, trying to smile.

159

Andrea

On the flight out, I kept trying to imagine the woman Louie was seeing in Santa Cruz. I saw her as short, because I'm tall, and blond, because I'm a brunette, and spunky, because I'm reserved, and maternal because I've fought the tendency all my life.

My mother was trying to kill herself, and all I could think about was losing Louie. Though the captain said we had a tailwind, it was an interminable flight.

27.

Eva, in her nightgown, was waiting at the front door when Louie arrived that evening. She ran down the path to the gate, told the Doberman to stop growling, then escorted Louie into the house.

Marie waved from the kitchen as Louie and Eva entered. She was preparing a late supper, smiling beatifically, as if she'd just discovered some wonderful, essential truth.

Eva led Louie upstairs to her room, where she proceeded to show him her various athletic outfits and her flute, guitar and bongos, which she couldn't play just then because Cal was asleep. With great ceremony she showed him her collection of match books, and then she got in bed and asked if he would please read her James Thurber's *Many Moons,* which was her favorite book in the whole world. Louie began to read it, but Eva fell asleep before he'd gotten past the second page.

He and Marie ate by candlelight. He told her about seeing Joanna, and about Helen's suicide attempt. Marie listened intently, encouraging him to talk, to tell her every detail. As he spoke, she made sure to keep his wineglass full.

After supper she served him Irish coffee and sat close beside him on the couch. He began to tell her about Andrea, but she silenced him with a kiss, slipped her warm hands under his shirt and told him what she wanted to do with him in bed.

Louie made an attempt to pull away, but when Marie whispered that she had been waiting for five years to make love to him, that she would die if he didn't take her to bed, that it was the only way he could make amends for leaving her, he let himself caress her.

They climbed the stairs together, stopping once to paw at each other. When they got to her room she undressed him, kissed his feet, his thighs, his cock, his belly and throat and face, and then she sat on the bed and hurriedly took off her clothes. She cupped her breasts with her hands and lay back, urging him with her eyes to come to her. When he hesitated, she said, "Come on, Louie. It's all for you."

When he came to the bed, she grabbed his hand and pulled him down on top of her, carefully touching his cock and guiding it into her. "Louie," she said, weeping. "You're finally in me, Louie."

He held her, not daring to move until she stopped crying, and then he tried to withdraw, but she held him

162

in her, tongued his ear and said roughly, "Come on, Louie. Don't run away. I want you."

He bowed his head and sucked gently on her breasts, then took hold of her buttocks and began to thrust into her. She raised her legs up high, allowing him to sink deeper into her, then moved with him, faster and faster, until he exploded inside her.

They lay quietly, locked together for several minutes. She tried to keep him in her, but he worried he was crushing her and rolled off. She kissed his mouth, then moved down him, kissing his throat and belly. She licked his cock until he was hard again, then straddled him, easing herself down onto him. She put her hands on his chest, he put his hands on her breasts, and she rode him for a long time, rocking back and forth, moving up and down, slowly at first, then faster, then slowly again.

"I love you, Louie," she whispered. "I want to give you everything. I want to have babies with you."

Louie pulled her down to him and kissed her cheek, changing their sex into an embrace. Then he rolled with her onto his side, pulling out of her as he did so. He held her close, his lips on her throat, his eyes shut tightly.

"What's wrong?" she whispered. "Tell me, Louie."

"It's nothing wrong with you," he said, pulling away slightly. "You're wonderful."

"Is it Andrea?" she asked, moving closer to him, massaging his back. "You want her more than me?"

"I told her I'd go back to Virginia with her," he said, his voice shaky.

"And will you?" she asked, gently.

"I don't think so," he said, looking at her. "I think I want to stay with you."

She kissed him and began to cry. "I can't help you there, Louie. I want you, but I can't decide for you."

She gave him a sorrowful look. "Don't do it out of guilt. Stay if you love me, if you want to be father to my kids."

"I have to see Andrea," he said, touching Marie's face. "I came to say goodbye to you, and now I have to say goodbye to her."

"Do you love her?" asked Marie.

"Yes," he said, nodding.

"But you love me more," she said, challenging him.

"I must," he said, "I'm choosing you."

"You're *with* me, Louie. You chose her when you were with her. Maybe you choose whoever chooses you."

"No," he said. "I've never had to choose like this before."

"Yes you have," she said, stiffening. "When you left, you chose yourself over me. I don't blame you now, but don't say you never had to choose."

Louie rolled onto his back and stared up at the ceiling. He groped for Marie's hand, found it and held it lightly. "I've never told anyone this," he said, sighing heavily, "but when I left Soledad, I . . . I went somewhere." He stopped speaking and sat up, his body trembling.

"Where, Louie?" she asked, sitting up with him.

"It's crazy," he said, shaking his head. "When I think of it now, I can't believe I did it, but I just couldn't stand your being in prison and my being free, so I . . . for a while, I just roamed around, trying not to think about you, but all I *did* was think about you, and finally I was in Santa Barbara, and I hadn't eaten anything for a long time, or slept, so I called the crisis number, and they told me to go to a hospital, which I did, and the doctor there suggested I admit myself to a mental hospital. So I did. I stayed in until you were supposed to get out of prison, and then I got out."

"Louie," she said, putting her arms around him.

"It was good for me," he said, calming down. "I felt okay after a few weeks, and then I wanted to stay. I wanted to help those people, to talk to them, to prove to myself I could put their needs above mine. I was sort of like a patient orderly. The doctors kept trying to discharge me, and I kept saying I couldn't leave until August twenty-fifth. I ended up staying for almost five months."

"Why didn't you come back after you got out?" she asked, lying back and pulling him down with her.

"I wasn't strong enough," he said, looking at her. "I needed to prove to myself I could be completely alone, without any money, with nothing, and still make it."

"And did you?" asked Marie, embracing him.

"Yeah," he said wistfully. "It's not much fun, but I can do it."

"Well, now you've proved it," she said, kissing him. "Now you can have fun again."

165

Eva

He was in Mom's bed, so I know they're in love. I went in before school and he opened one eye and growled at me. I asked him if he would be there when I got home from school, because Carol might come to meet him, but he said probably not. Then I asked him if he was going to marry Mom and he put his head under the covers.

So then I went downstairs for breakfast and when Cal left, I asked Mom if she was going to marry Louie and she said it was none of my business, but I think they are because she smiled and her face got red, so they probably are.

28.

Louie stopped in Watson-
ville to wash the Mercedes and fill it with gas before
taking it back to Pajaro. Then he stopped at a produce
stand and bought fruit and flowers for Andrea and
Helen. But when he approached the Pajaro gate, he
lacked the courage to go in. He pulled over to the side of
the road, got out of the car and walked across the
artichoke field to where the cement pipe overlooked the
river. The path he'd cut to the pipe had been enlarged.
When he looked inside, he was shocked to see his
sanctuary full of garbage, aluminum cans, broken bot-
tles and excrement.

He walked down the steep incline to the filthy river

and watched a flotilla of coots and mallards cruising the far shore. He wondered what they could possibly find to eat in the poisoned water. The sky was clouding over. He could smell the storm coming, but he was still afraid to go, afraid to see Andrea, so he stayed there watching the birds until drops of rain began to blister the glossy surface of the river.

By the time he reached the house, the rain was falling hard and he was soaked. Andrea opened the front door and Buka leapt up on him, slobbering happily. Andrea took the fruit and flowers from Louie, set them on the floor and put her arms around him.

"You trimmed your hair," he said, pulling back as she was about to kiss him.

"A kiss?" she said plaintively.

He kissed her tentatively, dryly, then pulled away, took her hand and led her into the living room. He sat in the rocking chair and she sat on the couch.

"Yes?" she said, watching him closely. "This feels momentous."

"How's Helen?" he asked sternly.

"Asleep," she said, about to cry. "And how are you? I missed you."

"I'll start a fire," he said, getting up.

"Would you like some wine?" she asked, bewildered by his behavior.

"No," he said, kneeling on the hearth. "Some tea, maybe."

When the fire was blazing, Louie returned to the rocking chair. Andrea brought him his tea, having poured herself a glass of red wine. She stood by the fire, looking down at the flames, waiting for Louie to say something.

"I've decided to stay in Santa Cruz for a while," he said, finally, sounding somewhat doubtful about it.

"For how long?" she asked, sipping her wine.

"Maybe permanently," he said, nodding.

"Do you want to tell me about it?" she said, turning to him. "I'd really like to know why."

"Well," he said, beginning to rock, "the woman I went to say goodbye to wants me to stay, and I think I owe it to her . . ."

"Louie," said Andrea, shaking her head, "tell me the truth."

"What do you mean?" he said angrily. "I *am*."

"Then don't make it her choice. Say what *you* want to do, not what she wants, not what you owe her."

"But I do," he said, his anger dissipating. "She needs me."

"And you must need her," said Andrea simply. "I need you, too. So what you're saying is that you prefer her to me. The rest is just rationalization, Louie. You want her instead of me."

"No," he said, looking out the window. "That's another one of the old lies." He turned back to her. "I love you both, and if I could, I would keep loving you both, but that's not allowed. I have to choose."

"I guess another lie is that if you really loved me, you wouldn't want her," said Andrea, sitting on the couch.

"I don't *want* anybody," Louie said sadly. "I want to love you, and I want to love her, and I don't mean sexually, I mean to care for you both."

"But you did sleep with her," said Andrea, finishing her wine.

"Yes," he said quietly.

"And was it nice?"

"It was terrifying," he said, stopping his rocking.

"But was it nice?" she asked again, getting up to refill her glass.

169

"It would take so long to explain," he said wearily. "I probably should just go."

"Wait for Helen to wake up," said Andrea, struggling to control herself. "She'll want to say goodbye."

"I'm sorry," he said, starting to rock again.

"It's my theory," said Andrea, ignoring his apology, "that you are incredibly close to not hating yourself any more. Getting rid of that last little bit of it must be almost impossible."

"I don't hate myself," he said weakly. "I just can't run away from her again."

"Look at yourself, Louie," Andrea said, coming close to him. "Look at how you're sitting, how you're holding yourself, how sad you are, and think about how you were with me, and tell me you're loving yourself now."

"It's not that simple," he said.

"I never said it was simple," she said, moving to the fire. "I've known very few people who have made the leap. But that's why I fell in love with you, because you were about to, and I wanted to leap with you."

"You're so fucking eloquent," said Louie, trying to sit up straight. "You and your mother."

"I'm right, too," she said, setting her wineglass on the mantel so she could hug herself to keep from trembling.

"Goddamn it," Louie whispered, curling his hands into fists, "I should have just left the car and gotten the hell out of here." He glared at her, then got up and went out onto the deck, in the rain.

Andrea went to the doorway and looked out at him. He was standing at the rail, his shoulders hunched, his head bowed. The rain was beating down on him, but he seemed oblivious to it.

"Are you leaving?" she asked quietly.

"No!" he shouted fiercely. "Just leave me alone."

170

Andrea

How did Androcles ap-
proach the wounded lion? That was one of Father's
bedtime questions for me as a child, and I would stay
awake for hours, trying to imagine how a little person
would approach a raging beast without being torn to
pieces. That was my dilemma with Louie. He wasn't
going to leave until we'd done something to relieve his
anguish, but he wasn't going to stay and be my devoted
friend unless I could get the thorn all the way out.

He came inside sniffling and miserable. I started the
shower and got out some dry clothes for him. He glared

at me the whole time, but finally went into the bathroom and locked the door.

Mother woke up in the middle of all this, got into father's wheelchair and rolled herself into the kitchen, where she started in again about wanting to die. She wanted me to help her, to let her go, which made me furious. Then Louie came in, glowering at both of us, so I poured myself another glass of wine and retreated to the living room, leaving them to argue with each other.

Louie always sounded so rational, so wise and understanding when he was dealing with other people's problems and sorrows, but he was such a dunce about himself.

I sat in the rocking chair listening to my mother explain in her maddeningly logical way why it would be better for her to die now, rather than wasting away, ruining my life as well as hers. I shouted to her not to worry about that, and she shouted back, "That's easy for *you* to say."

Louie wheeled her in by the fire and gave her a shoulder rub, which seemed to calm her down somewhat. I watched them for a few minutes, was about to say something snotty about their mutual myopia, but I caught myself and went into the kitchen to make dinner.

I was drunk and dizzy, arguing with myself about what to do, when I looked up and there was Louie, standing in the doorway, smiling at me, enjoying my lunacy, so I threw an onion at him and told him to go to hell.

29.

They ate a simple meal in the dining nook. Helen drank wine against the doctor's orders and refused to take her tranquilizer. Andrea pounded the table and told her mother she *had* to take it.

"I do not wish to be sedated," said Helen blithely. "I'm going swimming tonight and want to be very sharp when I do."

"Mother, please," said Andrea, gritting her teeth.

"But I may need some help getting past the breakers," said Helen, cocking her head to one side. "Big waves tonight. Did you see them, Louie?"

Andrea slammed down her fork. "I want you to stop talking like this, right now."

"Isn't the role reversal delightful," said Helen, tapping Louie's plate with her spoon. "We become the children to our children. If you don't let me go, you'll be changing my diapers before long, and I won't know enough to *want* to die."

"I don't want you to die, Mother," said Andrea, pushing herself away from the table, her forehead throbbing.

"I know you don't," said Helen, "and I appreciate that, dear, but you have to understand that your desire for me to keep on living is wholly selfish. It has nothing to do with me."

"What did you have in mind?" said Andrea, crushing her napkin. "That we swim out with you and let you drown?"

"No, darling," said Helen, reaching out to Andrea, "drowning is something that happens against our will. This is something I *want* to do."

"Well, I'm sorry," said Andrea, standing up, "but I can't help you."

"Will you stop me?" Helen asked, hopefully.

"Yes!" shouted Andrea, hitting the table with her fist.

"Then what's the point of trying?" said Helen, her shoulders sagging. "I'm a prisoner."

"Excuse me," said Andrea, leaving the room.

"You're pretty hard on her," said Louie, when Andrea was out of earshot. "We weren't taught to let people die, you know. It may be a good idea, but it's not easy to accept, especially with someone as intact as you seem to be."

"I'm impatient," said Helen, gulping her wine. "It's a fault, I admit, but she's so stubborn."

"And you're not!" said Louie, laughing.

"If I weren't her mother, I know she'd want to help me."

"You're more than her mother," he said, frowning. "You're her family. You're it."

"Which is where I thought you'd come in," Helen said, sighing and fluttering her eyelashes. "Oh, well."

"That's not fair," said Louie, shaking his head.

"Oh, it's *not* fair. We've established that. What I'm hoping for is some tiny bit of meaning. I do so hate the apparent meaninglessness." She touched Louie's hand. "George was my teacher, too, you see. But I'm not as strong as he, and if I'm to avoid becoming a victim of my own physical frailty, I have to act now, while I've got strength for death." Tears rolled down her cheeks, but she wiped them away and gave Louie a proud look. "Remember how weak George was, how inert. And look what he did. Don't you see, Louie, we *all* become victims when we let others decide for us."

"I decide," he said, looking away, ashamed.

"Forget about hurting other people, forget about letting them down. That's irrelevant." She took his hand. "Should I suffer along for another ten years, so people will think I'm a nice old lady? Should you choose a woman so she won't be hurt by your *not* choosing her? No. I'll die because I know it is the best thing for *me*. And you, I hope, will do whatever you do because you *want* to do it. In the end, we'll do much less harm being truthful, believe me, Louie. You have to have faith in the resilience of the survivors."

Helen

I went to my bedroom and wrote in my journal, trying to say it all in a few good paragraphs. Then I got out my boxes of photographs and looked through them all one more time.

Louie came in and sat on the bed, and I showed him pictures of Andrea when she was little, and pictures of me when I was younger than she is now.

After a long time, he said something that almost made me change my mind about going. He said that it would be wonderful if I were to live to see Andrea's children. The implication was, I'm fairly sure, that they would be his children too.

176

30.

Andrea was washing dishes, scrubbing them zealously, trying to work off some of her anger. Louie came down the hall from Helen's room and stood in the kitchen doorway, watching her.

"Shall I rinse?" he asked, moving toward her.

"Get away," she said, glancing angrily at him. "Go back to Santa Cruz."

Louie moved cautiously to the sink and began rinsing the dishes and stacking them in the drainer. When he'd rinsed all that she'd washed, he put his arms around her and kissed her. She kept her mouth shut tightly, her soapy hands away from him. He released

177

her, and she continued washing dishes as if nothing had happened. He watched her for a moment, then went back to rinsing until all the dishes were done.

"Why did you do that?" she asked, pouring herself a cup of coffee and carrying it into the living room.

Louie followed her to the couch, but didn't sit with her. Instead he squatted by the fireplace and put a big piece of driftwood onto the coals, waiting for it to ignite before answering her.

"I did it because I love you," he said, standing up, "and because I want to come with you. But if I do, I don't know how I'll ever be able to tell Marie."

"Come here," said Andrea, holding out her hand to him.

"I have to say this before I touch you," he said, staying where he was. "It may not work out for us. You might not like me a month from now. You might want somebody else more, or want to go somewhere I don't. Or I might fall apart, or run away, or come back out here. I can't promise anything except to try, and I won't even be able to do that if I can't get up the courage to face her. But I will *not* run away again." He put his hands in his pockets and leaned back against the mantel. "You might even want me to stay with her if you knew the whole story."

"Tell me," said Andrea, patting the couch beside her. "I'll bet I don't."

Andrea

When he finished telling me about Marie, I sat there thinking about her, worrying about her, wanting her to be happy, but never once thinking Louie should go back to her. But I understood why he was so afraid, why it had been easier for him to say goodbye to me than to her. Fear is often more powerful than love.

Then we went to bed, but we didn't make love. We talked about my mother and moving back to Virginia, and what my house was like, and my neighborhood, and my friends. And then I was so tired, so relieved that he was coming with me, I drifted off to sleep, and might have slept through the night if Buka hadn't awakened me.

179

31.

"Louie?" said Andrea, sitting up in bed, pushing her dog away. "Louie?"

She got up, went across the hall to Helen's room and turned on the light. On top of the neatly made bed was a metal box in which Helen kept her jewelry and important documents. On top of the box was an envelope. Andrea ran down the hall to the kitchen, calling out for her mother and Louie. Buka was at the back door, scratching at the glass. Andrea slid the door open and ran out onto the deck. The rain had stopped, but it was extremely dark. She went back inside and got a flashlight, then followed her dog down to the beach.

The tide was in, narrowing the beach to twenty yards of sand. Andrea pointed her beam of light northward, then to the south, and then she searched the waves with it, but she couldn't see anyone. Buka had run south. She jogged in that direction, clicking off the flashlight to preserve the batteries.

Buka ran for a good quarter of a mile and then waded out into the shallows, barking at something he saw in the waves. Andrea clicked on her light and pointed it out at the frothy water, the little beam illuminating almost nothing. She stood behind her dog and aimed the flashlight in the direction his nose was pointing, and there, at the far end of the light's range, she saw someone swimming. It was impossible to see who it was, but Andrea waded out, carrying the flashlight with her. When the water was up to her waist, she was forced to dive under a large wave. When she came up for air, the light had been extinguished and she could no longer touch bottom. She let go of the flashlight and swam out to where she thought the person must be.

The undertow was strong, carrying her out quickly to where the offshore current took over and pulled her southward. She was freezing cold and knew she couldn't last for long. She began to work her way in, riding the swells as best she could, swimming on her back in order to anticipate the incoming waves. After several minutes, she could feel herself growing dangerously tired, but she still couldn't touch bottom. A panic seized her and she began to swim frantically, using up the last of her strength. And then suddenly a huge wave lifted her to its crest and dumped her with incredible force. She was pushed down through several feet of water and tumbled roughly along the sandy bottom. She emerged, gagging and coughing, still unable to get a foothold on the sand. She screamed, her voice piteously weak admidst the roar and crash of the waves, but Louie heard her.

He was to the north of her, invisible in the darkness. He called to her, she shouted his name, and he appeared, swimming powerfully over the crest of a wave. When he got to her, he hooked his arm around her chest and together they kicked toward shore. Within moments they were able to touch bottom. They stumbled through the surf, collapsing together on the sand.

"Where's Mother?" asked Andrea, struggling to stand up.

"She's gone," said Louie, lying on his back, his chest heaving.

"Did you see her?" asked Andrea, dropping to her knees beside him.

"I swam out after her," he said, rolling over onto his stomach and pushing himself up onto his knees.

"Jesus," said Andrea, leaning against him and crying.

"It was amazing," he said, holding her tight. "She saw me coming and ran out into the water, diving over the waves, like it was easy for her. I tried to reach her, but . . ." He stopped to calm himself and catch his breath. "I got close, but she was far enough ahead of me to get over this one big wave before it broke. But I was in front of it, and it knocked me down and pushed me back to shore."

"But how did you find me?" she asked, sobbing.

"You must have run by me in the dark, because when I saw you run out with your light, you were south of me," he said, getting up and helping her stand. "We have to get ourselves warm, or we'll be sick."

"She's out there," said Andrea, pulling away from him.

"She's a better swimmer than I am," he said gently, taking Andrea's hand. "Let's run."

"Where's Buka?" she said, resisting.

"We have to get warm," he said, sternly.

"All right," she said, taking his hand.

They turned away from the ocean and ran, pulling each other along, back to the house.

Helen

Dear Andrea,

I think you'll find all my papers in order. I've left a letter for my sister. She's always wanted those dangly earrings from Thailand, so please see that she gets them.

I am immensely proud of you. You are all I ever hoped you would be, and more. I love you very much and wish for you a magical life. Please do not grieve too long for me. I am content.

32.

Marie was in her garden, planting out lettuce seedlings. She had a red bandanna tied around her forehead and was wearing old jeans and a well-worn chamois shirt. She stood up and leaned on her hoe when Louie came out into the backyard.

"Now there's a hangdog look if I ever saw one," she said, smiling radiantly at him.

He straightened up and took his hands out of his pockets. "I'm going, Marie," he said, making himself look at her.

She nodded, then dropped the hoe and fell to her

185

knees beside the baby lettuce. She poked a hole in the loose soil, fumbled for a seedling and lowered it into the ground.

Louie put his hands back in his pockets and walked toward her. "I'd like to stay in touch with you," he said, stammering slightly. "See how the kids are doing, how you're getting along."

She didn't say anything at first, but kept setting out the lettuce, taking care with the fragile roots. Then she looked up at him, her eyelids drooping, as if it were a struggle for her to stay awake. "How could we do that, Louie?"

"I don't know," he said. "We just will."

"We can't," she said, shaking her head.

"I care about you," said Louie. "I'm never going to stop caring about you."

"You better," she said, sighing to keep from crying.

"Why?"

"Quit asking why,, Louie," she said, glaring at him. "That's what three-year-olds do. Only they ask it because they want to know. You ask it to keep from answering it yourself."

"I'm sorry I ran away," he said, his eyes filling with tears.

"Well, you didn't run away this time," she said, standing up, dusting off her knees. "Thank you for that."

"I'd like to write to you," he whispered.

"Let it go, Louie," she said, coming close to him and putting a hand on his shoulder.

"I don't want to," he said, looking down and kicking the ground. "Why do we always have to let things go? Why can't things change?"

"There you go again," she said, backing away. "Asking why when you already know the answer."

186

"I don't *like* the answer," he said, looking at her.

"Tough shit, Louie," she said, turning away. "That's the way life is. Your problem is, you got too much woman in you."

"Now wait a minute . . ."

"No," she said, closing her eyes, "just get out of here. You keep waiting for some sort of resolution. It's been resolved. You made a choice."

"You're right," he said, nodding.

"If it helps, I forgive you," she said, quickly kissing him. "Goodbye."

"Goodbye," he said, turning away.

Eva was coming up the walk as Louie came out the front door. She was swinging her Snoopy lunchbox and singing "Frère Jacques."

"Are you crying?" she asked, looking wonderingly up at Louie.

"No," he said, sniffling. "Got something in my eye."

"It's okay for boys to cry," she said, frowning. "Are you?"

"Yes," he said, picking her up, holding her on his hip.

"Wait, wait!" she said, excited. "Can you do alley oop?"

"What's that?"

"Put me down, I'll show you," she said, dabbing his wet cheek with her finger.

Louie put her down. She set her lunchbox on the lawn, took off her sweater and rubbed her hands together.

"Okay," she said, her eyes wide with delight, "now cross your hands."

He crossed his hands.

"Your arms, I mean," she said, demonstrating. "Now stick out your knee like this."

187

Louie stuck out his knee and they clasped hands. She put her right foot up on his knee and looked him in the eye.

"Okay, now," she said gravely, "this is the hard part. On *alley*, you pull me up onto your knee, and on *oop*, you swing me up and around onto your shoulders."

"Okay," said Louie, closing his eyes. "But then I have to go."

Andrea

When Louie got back from Santa Cruz, he said if it was all right with me, he wanted to load the car and leave for Virginia right away, instead of waiting a day or so as we had planned.

We filled the car until there was just barely enough room for Buka to sit in the back seat, then we checked the house one last time, locked it up, coaxed the dog into the car, and left.

Louie was upset, but he didn't want to talk about it yet, so I didn't press him. He drove first, getting us to Sacramento by dark. I suggested we spend the night there and get a fresh start in the morning, but Louie wanted to go on.

We got gas, walked the dog, ate our sandwiches, and then I took a turn driving. We left the valley and climbed up into the Sierras, the old Mercedes straining under the load. Then just before we got to the state line, Louie asked me to pull over to the side of the road. I did, he got out and ran along the shoulder of the highway until he came to the boundary line.

He stared down at the stripe they'd painted across the road, then he backed up several yards, ran toward the line and leaped across it. Then he beckoned for me to come to him, because he did not want to cross back.

ABOUT THE AUTHOR

TODD WALTON lives in Northern California, in the thriving town of Sacramento. He is the author of *Inside Moves*, which was made into a motion picture, and *Forgotten Impulses*, for which he has written the screenplay. He is a gardener, a musician and a cat lover.